The Year
of the Horse

The Year
of the Horse

by Diana Walker

ABELARD-SCHUMAN

NEW YORK

Published simultaneously in Canada by Fitzhenry & Whiteside Limited, Toronto.
Manufactured in the United States of America

Library of Congress Cataloging in Publication Data

Walker, Diana.
      The year of the horse.

      SUMMARY: Fifteen-year-old Joanna had no interest
in horses, let alone competition riding, until she met a
horse named Horse and a boy named John.
      [1. Horses—Fiction] I. Title.
PZ7.W15233Ye   [Fic]   75-4613
ISBN 0-200-00151-5

10 9 8 7 6 5 4 3 2 1

To Martin and Mary Kempers
who taught me to ride,
and to Black Label, Spirit and Charm,
who cooperated—sometimes.

Books by Diana Walker

Never Step on an Indian's Shadow
The Year of the Horse

Contents

The Year
of the Horse

A Meeting and an Accident

· 1 ·

Grandma's barn is a great place to go when you feel like sitting and thinking. Perched on a rise overlooking the rolling farmlands of southwestern Ontario, it commands a view so peaceful and quiet that petty irritations get soothed away in no time at all, and in our family these irritations are the rule rather than the exception. I love my family but sometimes I think all of them except me are a little mad, and it is absolutely imperative that I have a place to escape to, where I can think thoughts that are slightly more elevated than how Julian's sodden, mud-stained shorts happen to be gracing the living room chesterfield, or whether Maxwell's hamsters are getting enough vitamin B in their diet.

I am halfway between fifteen and sixteen, and my name is Joanna Longfellow. I have a seventeen-year-old sister, Margaret, who wants to be a writer like my father, and who is always tearing up first chapters with dramatic, despairing gestures. I also have two brothers, Julian and Maxwell, who are twelve and eight, respectively. Julian hates his name, but Maxwell loves his. Wherever you go you see MAXWELL LONGFELLOW scrawled over walls, magazine covers, in the dust of roads in the summer and along snowbanks in the winter, so you can't ever get away from him completely, not even on solitary walks. My parents think Maxwell is brilliant, but there is such a fine line between genius and insanity, I think they are kidding themselves.

Mother is probably the sanest of the bunch but, with such weird children and a temperamental husband to cope with, she always looks slightly wild eyed, as though at any moment she might drop everything and start to scream. Maybe it's because of this that, whenever my father earns enough money with his freelancing to make us solvent, he sublets whatever city apartment we happen to be living in, unloads us on Grandma Tate and carts Mother off on a trip until the money's all gone. This makes for a very unsettled existence for us but, since we aren't consulted, we have to make the best of it. I have been to four schools in five years, and sometimes I have to think twice to remember which one I'm at currently.

In this particular spring we had been uprooted at Easter, while our parents took themselves off to Mexico, on a government grant, to study the Aztec Indians' eating habits, which made them live to be two hundred years old or something like that. I was despondent and resentful because I had fallen madly in love with the captain of the football team at my last school, and I hadn't even had a chance to make him aware of my existence. For the first time in my life, it occurred to me that my family didn't live like other people, and my future appeared dismal. I didn't see how I was ever going to have a lasting, meaningful relationship with anyone if I couldn't stay anywhere for more than six months.

Margaret and I were now attending the high school near Grandma's. It wasn't a bad school, but it seemed senseless to get involved in any extracurricular activities, when I didn't know how long I was going to be there. I used to think that all this moving around was fun, but now I was growing up, and desperately wanted to belong somewhere. I liked Grandma Tate and her old house in the country but, for the first time in my life, I couldn't get excited about being there. I didn't want to be moody; I couldn't help it. I tried to hide my feelings as well as I could, and the old barn helped. Whenever I felt like biting someone's head off, I fled to the solitude of the hayloft and felt sorry for myself in private.

The barn, the house and a couple of disintegrating tool sheds were all that was left of the Tate farm. When Grandpa Tate died, Grandma had sold all of her land—except for three acres—to the gentleman farmer next door. His name was Holmes and he was very rich. He worked in the city and came up on weekends, leaving his staff to run the farm. He bred show horses and had a prize herd of Holstein cattle— among other things—so, needless to say, he was not exactly in our social class. Grandma said he was very pleasant, but he didn't seem to be falling over himself to get to know us, and I didn't blame him. With a couple of little horrors like Julian and Maxwell around, it's best to stay clear, if possible.

The walls of the barn had been gradually stripped as old barn boards became popular for decoration, and now the barn was little more than a shell. Gently cooing pigeons flew in and out of the rafters and the hayloft was covered with debris, but the stone foundation was as solid as when it had been built over a hundred years ago. Perhaps I liked it so much because it had roots and I hadn't but, whatever the reason, I looked upon the barn as my own special place.

All around me was Mennonite country. The Mennonites are a religious sect, who had come from Europe in the last century and settled in Canada. Their way of life had hardly changed since then. They still wear dark old-fashioned clothing and use teams of horses to plow their fields and pull their little black buggies around the country lanes. Sometimes I envied them their changelessness, which showed how desperate I was. Mennonite girls my age must have little freedom, yet they looked content and happy, which is more than I could say for myself. I had half decided to leave home when I turned sixteen and find myself a job, but I didn't really want that either. I didn't know what I wanted—that was my trouble. Sometimes when I was alone I would find myself crying for no reason at all. My life seemed to be a mess of indecision and vague hopes that never materialized, and I could see it stretching on indefinitely with no bright spots anywhere.

The first holiday weekend, which came at the end of May, was a bad time for me. All the kids at school seemed to have something exciting planned, and I hadn't been asked to do anything. Margaret was busy on another first chapter, and had disappeared upstairs as soon as she got off the school bus. Julian and Maxwell had found themselves an after-school job, doing chores for some old farmer who lived nearby. Grandma was spring cleaning, and the house reeked of polish and lye soap. From upstairs came the thin whine of the vacuum cleaner. No one seemed to care whether I came home or not, so I helped myself to some chocolate cake and went to the barn to consider committing suicide. Once there, however, I realized that it wouldn't be any fun unless I could be around to see how sorry everyone was that I was no

4

longer among them, so I decided I would have to do something else. Meanwhile I was hungry and the cake was good.

Feeling better on a full stomach, I sat up and noticed that the chokecherry blossoms were beginning to fall. But the apple trees were coming out in pink frothy buds, and the grass was green and new looking. Killdeers swooped hysterically over the pond behind the barn and ran along the bank on stilt legs. A groundhog sat up very straight at the entrance of his burrow by the fence and eyed me saucily. It should be good to be alive, I thought wearily, if only I could discover the secret.

Then I saw something which really caught my attention. Over the hill, where the rail fence divided the Holmes's property, a horse and rider came into view. They paused for a moment on the crest, making a striking picture against the sky. As I watched, the rider jumped lightly from the horse and, letting it crop the grass, leaned on the fence, looking down at our house. I saw he was a boy not too many years older than myself.

Curious, I hung out of the loft as far as possible without falling on my face, and called out, "Hi! Do you want something?"

He turned in my direction, and I knew right away that he must be one of the Holmes clan. Both he and his horse absolutely oozed good breeding. You could see it in the bone structure of the boy's face, in the casual, expensive look of his clothes and the way his hair was cut, neither too long nor too short. My eagerness suffered a setback. I felt like a peasant beside him and I regretted my impulsiveness, but it was too late to retreat.

I had startled him. "Pardon?" he called back. His voice suited the rest of him. Instinctively, I tried to make myself

5

sound less like a foghorn, a characteristic I had developed over years of frustrated yelling at Maxwell and Julian, who could be stone deaf when it suited them.

"I just wondered if you wanted anything."

He smiled at me. "No thanks! I'm just looking around." Then he went back to contemplating our backyard clothesline, which was presently graced with a tattered rug and some seedy-looking underwear of Maxwell's. Someone like him had probably never seen a clothesline before. Still, I was a bit indignant that he seemed to be staring at it with such fascination. I felt he was not getting a fair impression of my family, and with the idea of diverting his attention to myself, I swung myself down to the ground and went up the slope to meet him. I was still wearing my red school dress, which looked nice with my long dark hair. I wished at that moment that I could have been beautiful, but at least my face wouldn't stop a bus, according to my father, who paid rather unusual compliments.

I gave him what I thought was a ladylike smile and said pointedly, "You seem very interested in my grandmother's house."

He got the message and looked embarrassed. "I'm sorry. I didn't mean to be nosy. Actually, I was thinking."

He looked preoccupied, even when he was talking to me. It was disconcerting but I persevered gamely.

"I'm Joanna Longfellow," I said in my best society voice. "How do you do?"

He looked startled again. No doubt he hadn't expected the peasants to have any kind of manners. "Hi, Joanna," he said with a stilted little laugh. "I'm John Holmes. Maybe you know my grandfather?"

"No," I said. "I haven't had that pleasure, but I've heard about him."

6

"Oh?" He looked amused for a moment. "Anything interesting?"

He had the edge on me, being naturally composed, whereas I was only putting on a big act. I felt my face redden. "Oh, I didn't mean anything like that!" I hastened to assure him, but that seemed to need an explanation, too, so I went babbling on stupidly, "I mean, I know he has pots of money and that Holmwood Farms is sort of a hobby with him and he raises prizewinning horses. . . ." Sometimes when I'm nervous I can hear my voice going on and on, saying absolutely nothing worth listening to. This was one of those times. I pulled myself up short and seized on the horse in an attempt to change the subject.

"Is that one?" I asked, giggling inanely. I put my hand through the fence to pat the horse's head, but it shied away from me and I nearly knocked out my front teeth on the top rail.

"Is this one what?"

"A prizewinning horse?" I mumbled. My society voice had fizzled away entirely by this time.

"This is Queenie," he said, patting her flank. "Her full name is Queen of the Nile. She has her share of red ribbons."

"She's beautiful," I said, really meaning it. I had never seen such a beautiful horse. Her mane and tail were blonde and she looked very aristocratic. She and John belonged together, and I was the odd one. I was getting more of an inferiority complex by the minute.

"Of course," said John with a short laugh, "everyone at Holmwood Farms, horses and people, have to be prizewinners. It's one of the rules. Maybe you heard that, too?"

I stared at him like a bumpkin. I didn't know if he was being sarcastic, snubbing me, or just politely putting me in my place for being nosy. My hackles rose. My family might be constantly living on a shoestring, but we do have a certain amount of pride.

"Actually," I said coolly, "we don't bother much with the people around here. We only stay here when my parents are traveling. My father's a writer, and he thinks country life is deadly boring."

That was one up for me. I was almost enjoying myself again. I saw I had aroused his curiosity. "Are you a large family?" he asked.

In an offhand manner I told him, "I have two brothers and a sister. My parents are in Mexico at the present time. Unfortunately, they couldn't take us with them because of school."

I stole a glance at him to see how he had taken that; he was staring at the ground, and I couldn't make out his expression.

"It must be nice to have a large family," he said at last. "You're lucky."

He was calling me lucky! I thought of Maxwell's frog spawn in the refrigerator which I had upset when I helped myself to cake, and I said fervently, "Oh, I wouldn't say that. Being an only child must have its good points."

He raised his eyes slowly. For a moment he had seemed quite human, but now he looked detached again, almost bored. "Maybe," he said shortly. "Well, I've got to be going. Nice talking to you."

I didn't know what to make of him. I was hurt and yet I was intrigued. "I guess I'll see you around," I blurted out. The disinterested approach was no good unless you had lots of time, which obviously I hadn't, and suddenly I did want to see him again, very much.

Swinging himself into the saddle, he looked down at me,

superbly aloof on his lofty perch. "Possibly," he said casually, "but I'm only here weekends and I spend most of my time training."

I wanted to ask him for what, but if that wasn't a brushoff my name wasn't Joanna Longfellow, and I do have my pride.

"Okay," I said, as though it were a matter of supreme indifference to me. "See you, then."

I turned and ran down the slope but, when I got to the bottom, I couldn't resist turning to see if he was still there. I caught a glimpse of him cantering over the rise, and then he was gone.

"Stuck-up beast!" I said to relieve my hurt feelings, but as soon as I realized he was a Holmes, I hadn't really expected anything different. He could get all the rich, beautiful girls he wanted, without slumming it with someone like me. But he had taken my mind off myself and given me something new to think about, and that was a good thing.

I went back to the house just as Grandma came down the stairs. She was a tiny bundle of energy with snow-white curls peeping wispily out from under a lopsided bandana.

"Goodness me, Joanna!" she exclaimed. "Is it that time already? Are the others home? I haven't begun to think about supper yet."

"That's all right," I told her. "We can have frankfurters. Margaret is upstairs writing the novel to end all novels, and the boys are over at Mr. Archer's. Would you like a cup of tea?"

She said that a cup of tea would be her salvation, so I made one for each of us.

"I've just been talking to John Holmes," I told her.

"Oh, he's such a nice boy," said Grandma. I should

9

explain here that Grandma likes everybody. The only person I've ever heard her criticize is Father, and that doesn't mean she doesn't like him.

"I thought he was a snob," I said.

Grandma was shocked. "Joanna, how can you say that? I hope you aren't mistaking good manners for snobbishness. He's always been so polite to me, the few times I've seen him. I know it's very fashionable nowadays for young folk to have Communist tendencies, but watch out you don't go too far."

Grandma comes out with the most amazing things at times. I think she watches too much television. I assured her that I wasn't about to become a threat to the Western world just because I thought John Holmes could do with being brought down a peg or two.

"Actually," I said wistfully, "there's nothing I'd like better than to be rich and have a nice normal family, with a father making millions on the stock market and attending PTA meetings and school concerts in a white Lincoln convertible."

Grandma tut-tutted at me. "Rich people have their misfortunes, too," she reminded me. "The Holmeses have had their share of trouble, goodness knows."

"Like what?" I asked with interest.

"Well, John's father lost a leg during the war. Before that he had been a championship rider. So had his father before him. Then John's mother died when he was quite small. So you see, riches can't guarantee happiness. It's up to John now to carry on the family tradition, and I hope for the sake of his father and his grandfather that he does well. I think they deserve it."

"I see," I said. Now I knew what John was training for, and why it was important, but I couldn't forget the look on his face when he had asked about my family. I tried to imagine what it would be like not to have a mother, and no brothers and sisters, and suddenly Margaret, Maxwell and Julian didn't seem so bad after all.

Grandma got up and rummaged through the leftovers in the refrigerator.

"That gruesome-looking blob of stuff in the plastic bowl isn't tapioca," I warned her. "That's Maxwell's frog spawn. I already spilled it once, so watch out."

"Oh, dear," sighed Grandma, removing it gingerly. "Why must he put it in the fridge? I'm sure it can't do those poor little tadpoles any good."

"Who knows?" I said. "Maybe he's experimenting so he can open a frog ranch in the Arctic Circle and sell frogs' legs to the Eskimos. How does anybody know how Maxwell's mind works?"

The object of our discussion entered at that moment, if you could call it entering. Actually he catapulted through the screen door with such force that the room shook. Julian, hot on his heels, narrowly missed having his face flattened by the rebounding screen door.

"Guess what? Guess what?" Maxwell was screaming.

"Maxwell," I sighed. "We're not deaf."

"Yes, but guess what? Old Mr. Archer fell out of a tree and broke his back!"

Grandma sat down limply, holding a package of frankfurters like a gift offering. "Maxwell, what are you saying?" she gasped.

"It's true," confirmed Julian. "There's this elm, you see, that died of Dutch elm disease and it's right over his barn, and Mr. Archer thought that the limbs ought to be cut off in case they crashed through the barn, so he went up to do it himself, and he slipped and fell off."

11

Grandma paled visibly. "Oh, how awful! That's terrible!"

"He's not dead or anything," Maxwell reassured her. "We phoned for an ambulance, and they took him to the hospital. He was conscious. He asked me and Julian to look after his place while he's away, because he trusts us. He doesn't trust anyone else," he added darkly, glaring at me as if daring me to contradict him.

"But how can you and Julian look after a farm while you're at school?" I objected. "That's a full-time job."

Maxwell eyed me pityingly. He always expects me to know everything without being told. "All he has is one horse, and all he grows is hay, and that doesn't have to be cut until fall."

"He has some chickens and ducks," corrected Julian.

Maxwell shrugged, writing off chickens and ducks as of no consequence, when compared with a horse.

"But I thought he was a farmer," I said.

Grandma, recovering gradually, said, "He was once, dear, but he's retired now. He's over seventy and lives on his pension. He's such a nice man."

"Then why do Maxwell and Julian go over every night?"

"Because he likes us, of course," said Maxwell, disgusted with my stupidity. "Besides, he trusts us with his horse."

"I don't know why he trusts you with his horse when you can't even look after your own hamsters," I said. Maxwell's hamsters were a sore point with me, since it always seemed to be me who got stuck with the job of cleaning out their cage. "What's so special about his horse, anyway?"

"His horse is a friend," Maxwell said with dignity. "Mr. Archer says you couldn't have a better friend in the whole world than a horse, if you treat it right. He's had a horse ever since he was six. He says a horse and buggy is better than a 'damfool' car any day. He says he wouldn't have a 'damfool' car if you gave him one."

"And you're supposed to look after the horse while he's in hospital, is that it?"

"It won't be any trouble," Julian pointed out. "She's out in the field. She's got a pond for water. All we have to do is talk to her, so she won't feel lonely. She just needs to be talked to sometimes and given treats. She likes treats. Her name is Horse. She's great."

I stared at him and made a great show of poking out my ears, but I had heard right. "A horse called Horse!" I exclaimed. "You've got to be kidding!"

Grandma had gone into the hall to telephone the hospital. While she was out, Margaret wandered into the kitchen. Her dark hair was frizzed up into a rat's nest where she had run her fingers through it in agonies of inspiration. There was also a pencil stuck in it somewhere like a left-hand directional signal.

"What's up?" she asked, bringing herself down to earth with an effort.

"Mr. Archer fell out of a tree, and they've taken him to hospital," I told her, "and Julian and Maxwell have custody of a horse called Horse."

"Oh, that's too bad," said Margaret sympathetically, but whether in reference to Horse or Mr. Archer I don't know, because she asked immediately afterward, "Why would anyone want to give a horse a stupid name like that?"

Maxwell was indignant. "It's not stupid! It's a habit. Mr. Archer was an orphan when he was six years old, and he went to live on a farm where there were five other kids and all sorts of cousins and things, an' it was bad enough

13

remembering the names of people so they didn't call the animals anything. They just said, 'Buckle up the horse' or 'Milk the cow' or 'Feed the donkey,' so it's just a habit with him now. He's always called his horses Horse. It saves him having to remember names."

That seemed reasonable after a fashion, but I was thinking of another horse with a beautiful name. I dropped it into the conversation casually. "I was talking to John Holmes this afternoon by the fence. *His* horse is called Queen of the Nile."

Margaret goggled at me. "You were talking to him?" she said with something like respect. "I saw him last year when Dad took me to the Royal Horse Show. He was riding Queen of the Nile then. She's beautiful. I was sure he would win something with a horse like that, but he didn't even place. I heard people saying it was his fault, but I don't understand how they're judged anyway. They all look good to me. What's John Holmes like? Is he snooty?"

"He's okay," I said, shrugging, but my mind was digesting this new information. So there had been one time when a Holmes hadn't been a prizewinner, whatever John Holmes had told me.

"I guess he must have had an off day," Margaret said generously.

"Yes, I guess he did," I agreed. The thought cheered me. Maybe John Holmes was human after all. I knew all about off days myself.

Grandma came back into the kitchen and informed us that Mr. Archer had broken his hip and two or three ribs, but was resting nicely. Bad though it was, it didn't seem as bad as Maxwell's first hollow pronouncement that Mr. Archer had broken his back, and such is human nature that we all felt warmly grateful suddenly, as though we were celebrating something.

"Now you boys be sure and take good care of that poor man's horse while he's in hospital," Grandma ordered them sternly.

They didn't have to be told. They were already puffed up with pride at their new responsibility, and taking it very seriously.

As for me, my thoughts kept straying elsewhere. The horse I was interested in at the moment was Queen of the Nile of the proud gait and spirited eye. And that only because she belonged to John Holmes of Holmwood Farms who rode into my life like a medieval knight and, suddenly, gave me a new zest for living.

Introduction to Horse

· 2 ·

The next day when Julian and Maxwell announced that they were going over to Mr. Archer's place, I decided to go with them. We set off after lunch, trailed by Grandma's old dog, Butch. His chief delight was sleeping but, about twice a year, he took a walk and this was one of those occasions. Instead of going around the roads, we took the shortcut over the fence that separated Grandma's property from the Holmes's farm.

Mr. Holmes owned over a hundred acres. All the fields were neatly defined by white fences, and the house, set among trees on a hill, was an impressive structure of fieldstone. Below it were the paddocks and farm buildings. Everything looked expensive and efficient even from a distance and, as we shoved Butch through the bottom rungs of the fence, I was overcome by a feeling of inadequacy and wondered how I had got up the nerve to speak to John Holmes yesterday. I would have preferred not to trespass, but there was nobody about, so I followed after the boys, keeping my head down as though in some way this would make me invisible.

In the lower pasture, several sleek horses were grazing with their foals. They had the same aristocratic stamp as Queenie, but I didn't see her among them. We climbed another fence into a plowed field, and a dip in the land hid us from the house, so I could relax.

"Do you always come this way?" I asked Julian. "Supposing somebody sees you?"

"So what? We're not doing anything wrong."

I wished I had the supreme confidence of a twelve-year-old again.

Mr. Archer's house was directly across from Holmwood Farms. Its architecture was ancient unpainted Ontario clapboard, a gloomy square box with a steep peaked roof. The driveway was lined with evergreens that had seen better days. Most of the lower branches were dead. There was a barn at the back in not much better condition than Grandma's, except that it had walls. After my distant view of John's house, this place depressed me utterly. It suggested failure, and seemed to mock my own desire to be somebody and make something of myself, as if it were saying to me, "Why bother? It all comes to this in the long run."

"What a miserable place," I said, as we walked up the driveway under the skeleton trees.

Maxwell was genuinely surprised. "What do you mean? I think it's terrific. Boy, I wish I lived here!"

His enthusiasm made me sad, because I knew that a year ago I would have found this tree-sheltered old house as exciting as he did. I would have been the first to want to explore it but, on this particular day, that sort of thing seemed childish and silly to me.

"Where's the horse?" I asked impatiently.

Overnight, because of John Holmes, I had become acutely interested in horses. I could still see him, so poised and confident on Queenie's back, and in my mind's eye I had transposed us, so that it was John looking up at me, envying me and longing to be my friend. I, of course, spurned him and galloped away, leaving him to trudge home, lonely and heartbroken, on his own two feet. It was a ridiculous but satisfying daydream. However, I had a real live horse at my disposal now. If I could learn to ride I would have something in common with John Holmes on which to base a friendship. I was determined about one thing. Horse would have to be rechristened. I would never be able to feel aloof and regal riding a horse with the prosaic name of Horse.

We crossed the sun-baked yard at the back of the house, disturbing some neurotic chickens and waddling ducks at the edge of a muddy pond. The back field was fenced, and there was a crude shelter of split rails at the far end.

"She'll be in there," said Julian. "The flies bother her."

Uttering sounds which I took to be intimate horse noises, he and Maxwell vaulted the fence and crossed the field. I followed some distance behind. A brown muzzle appeared around the edge of the shelter, followed by two limpid eyes under black bangs. Someone had cut the horse's forelock straight across her eyes, and it gave her a coquettish appearance. She gave a low whinny of pleasure at the sight of us and emerged at a slight trot. At once my dreams crumbled, for this horse was no more like Queenie than I was like John Holmes. She had a sweet face, and she was a nice light reddish-brown with a black mane and tail, but her proportions were hopelessly wrong. She had a round body and short, sturdy legs. She looked capable of pulling heavy loads

18

all day long, but as a silhouette against the sky she would be a disaster. I felt that if I sat on her my legs would drag on the ground.

The boys had brought apples and sugar. She nosed in their pockets and butted her soft nose against their chests, while I tried to reconstruct my shattered dreams.

"Why is she so funny looking?" I asked, my voice heavy with disappointment.

"What do you mean?" demanded Maxwell, outraged. "She's lovely. She's a small Quarter horse. Look how powerful she is." He ran his hands possessively over her flank, and Horse gave a little sigh and leaned on him. I thought she was going to fall over.

"What's a Quarter horse?" I asked, suddenly realizing how ignorant I was.

"A sprinter," Julian informed me, sounding very knowledgeable. "It has a terrific burst of speed for short distances, about a quarter of a mile, that's why it's called a Quarter horse. It's very sturdy and dependable and is used a lot on ranches for rounding up cattle. They're bred for polo ponies, too. Horse is a small one, but she's got a lovely disposition."

I looked at Horse and Horse looked back at me with her velvet eyes, and something inside me melted. Maybe she wasn't Queen of the Nile, but a Quarter horse was better than no horse at all, and I liked the bit about polo ponies. After all, polo was the sport of kings, so there must be more to her than met the eye.

"Can I ride her?" I asked.

Julian and Maxwell pulled faces at each other. It was humiliating to be at their mercy but, after all, Horse was their charge, and I would need to learn from them some of the finer points of staying on her back.

"S'pose so," said Julian, without much enthusiasm. "Not bareback, though. You'd fall off for sure. Better find the saddle, Max."

While this exchange was going on, I showed admirable self-control, even though I was longing to box their ears. Maxwell took off for the barn, and Horse, deprived of her leaning post, tried using me instead, but I wasn't having any of that. Julian, holding her halter, said, "She's very affectionate."

"I wouldn't call it affection," I said. "I'd call it plain laziness, or maybe she just had a late night."

Maxwell returned with a heavy western saddle draped over one arm, and a bridle on the other. The saddle leather was darkened with age and cracking. It seemed a shame it had been so neglected, but when I remarked about this to Julian, he replied scornfully, "Nobody uses it around here. It hasn't been used for years. Max and I ride bareback."

I clenched my teeth, refusing to let him make me feel like a freak just because I wasn't prepared to jump blindly on a naked horse and, clutching its neck, go galloping madly around the field. "The best people have some riding style," I told him haughtily. "They wouldn't be caught dead bareback."

Unimpressed, Julian and Maxwell sniggered. I don't know whether Horse sniggered, too, but she didn't take kindly to being saddled up. She kept shying away from the bit, but at last they got it between her teeth and the saddle girth around her ample middle.

"Hey!" I cried in protest. "Aren't you pulling that too tight? You're going to split her in two."

"Horses are crafty," Julian informed me, impatient with my stupidity. "They swell themselves when the girth is tightened, then let the air out so the saddle will be nice and loose, but that's no good. It'll just slip around, as soon as you get on it, so you've got to pull the girth real tight. It doesn't hurt."

Both of them were tugging on the girth. I couldn't stand it. "Look," I said firmly, "that horse is turning blue in the face. Leave it, will you? That's fine."

Julian shrugged. "Okay, if that's the way you want it. You're riding her, not me."

Patronizingly, they showed me how to place my foot in the stirrup and clutch strategic parts of Horse and saddle for the leap up. It wasn't graceful on my part, but I clawed my way up somehow, and there I was sitting on a horse and feeling already one of the glamorous horsey set to which John Holmes belonged.

"Horse is very docile," Julian was saying. "She's too fat, that's her trouble. She doesn't get enough exercise, and she's very lazy, so you don't have to worry about her running away with you. Just prod her flanks gently with your heels and she'll start."

I tried it and it worked. We ambled around the field with a gentle undulating movement at about two miles an hour. It was very relaxing, and my confidence grew in leaps and bounds.

"Hey!" I cried. "How am I doing?"

"Don't slump so," said Julian. "You look like a sack of potatoes."

I knew I shouldn't have asked him. I gave Horse another experimental little kick, and she began to trot. She had a nice easy gait, and there seemed to be nothing to this riding business.

Maxwell was running beside me screaming, "Don't bounce! Stop bouncing! You look terrible!"

"Oh shut up!" I yelled, breathless with the effort of hanging on. "I'd like to see you doing so well!"

And then the saddle began to slip! It went so slowly that, unlike most accidents, I had time to think while it was happening. I wondered in a detached sort of a way whether I would be crushed to death beneath the horse's hooves, or dragged by the stirrups until I was raw and bleeding, and all the time the saddle kept sliding sideways and there was absolutely nothing I could do about it. As it happened, I was neither crushed nor dragged when I parted company with Horse. She stopped immediately, looking quite ludicrous with the saddle gracing her stomach, and began to crop grass. Fate had been good enough to deliver her of her burden, and she was not going to question the whys or wherefores of her good fortune.

Julian and Maxwell came running up and pulled me to my feet. "You see," said Julian. "You wouldn't listen to me. Are you okay?"

I felt myself gingerly. There was blood on my face. I had cut my forehead on a stone, and my appearance was not improved by having fallen into a swampy depression in the field, but I appeared to be in sound condition.

Maxwell said, "You'd better get up and ride her again at once. Otherwise you'll lose your nerve. You always have to do that when you fall off."

"I'll tighten the girth properly this time," simpered Julian.

I was indignant. "Can't you see I'm bleeding? I've got to go home and get cleaned up. I'll come tomorrow."

"You'll lose your nerve," predicted Maxwell again with gloomy relish. "It's a well-known fact."

"Not to me it isn't!" I retorted irritably. I had had

enough of them for one day. It didn't make me feel any better that I should have listened to Julian. I knew I was being a bad sport, but I was too disgruntled to care. I left them to their precious horse and headed for home. I had pulled a muscle in my leg when I had fallen so awkwardly. It began to ache with every step. I didn't want to trespass again on the Holmes's property, but I couldn't bear the thought of going the long way around. I hobbled over the first field and climbed the rise, and who should I see cantering straight toward me on Queenie but John Holmes? There was no way he could avoid seeing me. I froze, conscious of how awful I must look, covered with mud and blood, like something out of a horror movie.

He reined up sharply at the sight of me. "Good grief!" He chuckled. "What happened to you?"

"I was riding," I said haughtily, "and I was thrown." It sounded better that way.

"You didn't tell me you rode," he said. He vaulted out of the saddle and inspected the cut on my face. "You should get that cleaned up," he said. "Are you hurt anywhere else?"

"I've pulled a muscle in my leg," I told him, beginning to enjoy myself. I rather liked being the object of his concern. "I can't walk very well."

"If you can get up on Queenie," he said, "we could ride back to my place. There's a first-aid kit in the tack room."

I couldn't believe this was happening to me, but who was I to question the workings of fate? I was a bit awkward mounting, this being only the second time I had been on a horse, but I used my leg as an excuse. It was wonderful sitting high up on Queenie's back with John's arm around me. I completely forgot what a sight I must look.

"Were you jumping?" he asked me.

"Huh?" It took me a minute to collect my thoughts, then I said hastily, "No, not really. I was just sort of—er—breaking in this horse, and it threw me."

"Is it your horse?"

I would have liked to tell him it was, but there was a limit to how far the truth could be stretched. "No," I said. "It belongs to a friend of ours. We're not here often enough to have our own horse. We mostly live in the city."

"Too bad," he sympathized. "How's your leg feeling?"

"It's aching quite a bit," I said. I hoped that would explain why I was sitting kind of tensely in the saddle. It was an English saddle, with nothing to hold on to when we went up and down the hilly fields.

"You'd better keep off it for a while," he said.

It was nice to be told by him what to do, as though he really cared about me. I glowed under my muddy exterior and tried to look suitably helpless to arouse his protective instincts.

We came down through the paddocks and stables to the large barn. John dismounted and helped me down. There were two men in the exercise ring putting a skittish horse through its paces. One of them called out to John, "Your dad's looking for you!" Both of them eyed me curiously, wondering, no doubt, where John had picked me up.

"He can wait!" John's mouth was curiously tight as he gave me an arm for support. "Come on, Joanna, let's get you fixed up."

We went through a door in the big barn into the tack room. It was small and cozy, smelling of saddle soap and leather. The walls were lined with pegs for hanging saddles and bridles, and there was a sink in one corner. A couple of spaniels shared a horse blanket with a family of kittens on the floor, where sunlight streamed through the grubby window.

It was a friendly, earthy place, and I felt quite at home there. I had not imagined Holmwood Farms would be like this. I had thought it would be all antiseptic and highly polished, and I had been a bit afraid of it.

John sat me down beside the sink and went to work on me. He was very tall and lean and capable. I liked the way his dark-brown hair fell in a wave over his forehead. He put a Band-Aid on my cut, which had turned out to be superficial after all, and gave me a bottle of liniment for my leg. "That stinks," he said, "but it's good."

I was about to thank him, when the door opened and a man came in. I knew at once it was John's father because of the stick he carried, and one leg dragged slightly, although he didn't seem particularly hampered by his disability.

"Oh, so there you are!" he said to John. I could see he was angry. "When I say two o'clock, I mean two o'clock! I've been waiting half an hour for you already. When are you going to learn some discipline? Maybe you think you don't need any more training," he added with cutting sarcasm.

A slow flush mounted John's face. "Sorry," he said in a tight voice. "I was delayed."

For the first time, Mr. Holmes noticed me. "Who's this?" he demanded.

"She lives next door." John's expression was stony and defiant. "She was thrown from her horse, and I took a few minutes off to help her. Is that so awful? A half hour won't make much difference to whether I get a gold medal or not, will it?"

I would never have dared to talk to my father in that tone of voice. The atmosphere in the tack room had changed. It was not cozy anymore. It seemed to be crackling with sparks. For a moment, I almost thought John's father was going to hit him with his stick, he looked so angry, but he controlled himself with an effort and asked me if I was badly hurt. When I shook my head, too uncomfortable to speak, he turned back to the door sharply. "Get Jim to take her home in the wagon," he said as he went out. "Then perhaps I might have you in the ring, John, if it isn't too much trouble!"

I didn't know where to look when he was gone, I was so embarrassed. John was white about the lips as he turned back to me. "Sorry about that," he said in a strained voice. "My father forgets sometimes I'm not still ten years old. I'll get you a ride home, okay?"

He was gone before I could thank him. Sitting alone with the dogs and the cats, I felt bewildered and confused. I was used to quarrels in our family, but there seemed to be something deeper than a mere quarrel in the hostile way that John and his father had faced one another. Whatever it was, it disturbed me and did not fit at all into my idea of how life at Holmwood Farms should be.

After a while the door opened and Jim came in. He was the man who had spoken to John from the ring. He had a rough, kind face, and his smile was friendly. I liked him at once.

"Wagon's out front, sweetheart," he told me. "Can you make it on your own, or do you need a hand?"

I couldn't see any point in playing up my injuries now that there was nobody here to impress, so I told him I was fine.

As we drove down the curving driveway, I looked back to see if I could see John, but the house hid the stables from view. I wondered sadly if I would ever get another chance to speak to him. With my usual rotten luck, nothing seemed more unlikely at that moment.

Enter Mr. Crossley

· 3 ·

For a brief moment I had been part of the world of horses and horsemen, and I was hooked. Whether I ever saw John Holmes again or not, I knew I wanted to ride more than anything else in the world.

As soon as my leg was better, I started to go with Julian and Maxwell whenever they visited Horse. They were good kids really. When they saw that I was serious about riding, and had stopped making snide remarks about Mr. Archer's place and his beloved horse, they helped me all they could. They didn't know much, of course, but I did get some pointers from them. I learned how to groom and handle a horse, and how to use my knees for balance so that I wasn't always jerking the reins and grabbing handfuls of mane. By the end of the week I was cantering around the field like an old pro, hanging on for dear life but not once falling off.

Grandma went to visit Mr. Archer one afternoon in her

1950 model Ford. She never drove above twenty miles an hour—she was afraid that some vital part of the car might fall off if she started speeding along at thirty. The hospital was twenty miles away, in the market town of Kitchener. Grandma must have caused a lot of motorists to age prematurely, but she made it there and back and informed us that Mr. Archer was doing nicely. He was still under sedation, but he had inquired after Horse and was relieved to know she was all right. From the optimistic way she spoke, we somehow came to the conclusion that Mr. Archer would be home soon. The boys were sure he would let me go on riding Horse, because she needed as much exercise as possible. So the future looked rosy, and my life had taken on a new purpose.

In one week I had quite fallen in love with Horse. She had charm. I must have abused her a lot, unintentionally, when I was learning to ride, but she never held it against me. If she felt I was being too rough on her, she just stopped dead and looked round at me reproachfully. She never bucked me off as she would have been quite justified in doing, and she always welcomed me with a little whinny of pleasure as though I were her best friend. She did this with everybody, but it was nice all the same.

I could hardly wait for Saturday to come around again. The boys and I hurried through our weekend chores. We still used Holmwood Farms as a shortcut to Mr. Archer's, but I was getting used to it. As we ran up the driveway of the old house, we noticed a little red sports car parked outside the front door. We were surprised, but we had no feeling of foreboding then.

"I expect it's someone he knows come to check everything's okay," I said.

As I spoke, a man came around the side of the house and

smiled at us. I didn't like the look of him much. He was too red and beefy and, although he showed a lot of teeth when he smiled, his eyes didn't crinkle at all.

"You must be the kids who are looking after the horse," he said.

Maxwell and Julian eyed him suspiciously. They were always suspicious of strange adults. Maxwell, who is not a bit shy, asked boldly, "Who are you?"

"Who am I, little fellow?" The man's eyebrows arched slightly. "I'm Mr. Crossley, Mr. Archer's nephew. I'm taking care of his business." He ran his eyes shrewdly over Mr. Archer's run-down estate. "Nice bit of property he has here, if it were fixed up."

If he had wanted to make an enemy of Maxwell, he couldn't have chosen a better way than by calling him "little fellow." Maxwell was small, but he had perfected a withering look that was devastating. "Mr. Archer likes it just the way it is," he said coldly.

Forestalling trouble, I cut in hastily. "How is your uncle?"

Mr. Crossley turned to me, with relief I thought. "Much better. He should be discharged by the end of next week. He'll be convalescent for a while yet, but my wife is a nurse so we'll be taking him in with us. It just remains for me to settle things up around here. Then we'll see what's to be done about the place."

We stared at him, our faces blank. "You mean he won't be coming back!" I blurted out. "But what about Horse!"

"Ah yes, the horse! I'm glad you turned up because I wanted to see you about that." Speechless with shock, we watched him produce a wallet from his pocket. "I owe you some money for looking after the horse, and if you wouldn't mind coming over for another week, I'd be grateful. I have a friend who's interested in buying the horse for his son, but I won't be able to get the loan of a horse trailer until next weekend. How much do I owe you?"

Maxwell was purple in the face. "You don't owe us nothing!" he exploded. "You can't sell Horse! Mr. Archer would never let you!"

Mr. Crossley tried to look indulgent. I hoped he wasn't going to try patting Maxwell's head. Maxwell would have attacked him. "Be sensible, sonny. Mr. Archer is seventy-two. It's lucky that accident didn't kill him. Let me figure out what's best for him, eh? Now, let me see, would ten dollars be all right?"

"We don't want your old money!" spat out Maxwell contemptuously, but Julian, who was less sentimental where money was concerned, grabbed it hastily.

With that off his mind, Mr. Crossley again looked relieved. "I have to see about the chickens and ducks yet," he told me, "but that shouldn't be any problem. I'll let them go at a good price to some local farmer." He handed me a business card. "If you know anyone who might be interested, tell them to give me a call, will you?"

He was already squeezing himself like an outsized sardine into his little car. As he took off in a cloud of dust, we stared after him, stricken. Maxwell was so angry, he ground his teeth. "You shouldn't have taken that money!" he roared at Julian.

Julian was as dismayed as we were, but he was more practical. "Well, not taking it wouldn't have made any difference," he growled. "And we can always use money."

We were too upset to argue. We fed the chickens and gave Horse her treats and groomed her, but we were sick inside and nobody felt like riding. We walked home in dark silence, impatient to spill out our resentment to Grandma.

"Mr. Archer would never give permission to sell Horse!" declared Maxwell, while we were having lunch. "He's doing it behind Mr. Archer's back. He'll just die when he finds out Horse is gone. He made us promise to look after her."

Grandma tried to reason with us. "The poor man probably hasn't any choice, children. Mr. Archer isn't going to be able to look after himself for a long time, maybe never again. I think it's very kind of his nephew to take him in. Some people can't be bothered burdening themselves down with us old folks. They'd just put him in a home and forget about him. At least Mr. Crossley isn't that sort, and you say he has found a good home for Horse."

"He wants to keep the money for selling her. That's why he's doing it secretly!" scowled Maxwell.

"Now, Maxwell, that's not nice!"

"Well, why doesn't he leave her where she is, then? We'll take care of her until Mr. Archer gets back."

"But I'm telling you, dear, Mr. Archer may not be able to come back. He's not getting any younger, and that fall won't have helped him. Besides, you don't know how long you're going to be staying with me. I don't think you're being at all fair to Mr. Crossley."

We groaned in unison. I took Mr. Crossley's card out and was going to tear it into a million pieces, but Margaret asked to see it. Studying it intently, she said, "Aha!"

"What do you mean—aha?" I said irritably.

"He's in real estate," she said darkly. "I bet he wants to get his hands on that farm and sell it so he can make himself a big fat commission."

"But he couldn't do that!" I cried, alarmed.

"Yes he could. If he sold Horse and the other livestock while Mr. Archer's in hospital, there wouldn't be any reason for Mr. Archer to go on staying there when he came out. It would be too late for him to do anything about it then, poor old man. I expect he'd be glad to sell it."

"Oh, you don't think so, do you?" I gasped. I didn't like Mr. Crossley, but I didn't think anyone could be that mean.

Margaret shrugged. "Well, like I say, he'd get a big fat commission, if he sold the house for Mr. Archer, and Mr. Archer would get the money for the sale, probably about forty thousand dollars with all that land, so he'd be worth quite a bit. I bet they wouldn't take him in if all he had was his pension."

"But Mr. Archer would hate him if he sold Horse!"

Margaret pulled a face. "Oh, Mr. Crossley would probably say he was doing it with the best of intentions, with his uncle's welfare at heart, and all that sort of baloney, you know."

Grandma had had enough of Margaret's inventive imagination. "You don't know anything about it!" she declared firmly. "You're making this man out to be a villain, when he's only trying to do what he thinks best. If Mr. Archer isn't able to live alone anymore, it's kinder to sell Horse behind his back so it'll all be done with when he comes out. You can't keep a horse in the city. She'd have to be sold in the end, anyway. I don't want to hear any more of that kind of talk!"

We looked down at our plates in silence. Maybe Grandma was right, but we didn't want to hear Mr. Crossley being whitewashed. We wanted him to be the villain because we loved Horse and were about to lose her. We felt so miserable, we had to blame someone.

Grandma got up from the table and began clearing the plates away. "Cheer up," she said, trying to comfort us. "You must learn to take the rough with the smooth in this life. I know you've grown fond of Horse, but if Mr. Archer isn't back by the time your parents come home, what's to become of her? I know it's sad, but you have to be realistic."

"I don't want to talk about it anymore," I said. I was nearly in tears. Just as I was beginning to enjoy riding, it was all going to end. We could never afford a horse of our own, and if we could, we would never be anywhere long enough to keep it.

I went upstairs and sat on the bed, gloomily contemplating the wallpaper. Soon I heard Julian and Maxwell come thundering up the stairs after me. They slept in the glassed-in sleeping porch off my bedroom. Bursting into the room, they came to an abrupt halt at the bottom of the bed. Julian said diffidently, "Can we talk to you, Joanna?"

I knew when they had to stoop to being polite, they needed my help badly, but I wasn't really in the mood for them. "Well," I said, "I'll have to consult my appointment book, but I think I could squeeze you in somewhere between five and six."

"Oh, come off it, Jo!" said Julian, reverting to type. "It's about Horse."

"There's nothing else to say about Horse," I said miserably. "It's all been said."

"No it hasn't," declared Maxwell. "We don't think it's right to sell her without Mr. Archer knowing, whatever Gran says, even if Mr. Crossley does mean well."

"So," added Julian, "we think we ought to stop Horse being sold, until Mr. Archer's fit enough to decide for himself whether he's going back to live in his house again, or not."

"Well, exactly," I said, "but who's going to listen to us? We don't have any say in the matter at all."

"What if we hid Horse until Mr. Archer could make up his own mind what he wants to do?"

My jaw must have dropped an inch as I stared at Maxwell. "You mean *steal* her?"

"We wouldn't be stealing her," cut in Julian quickly, "because we've got an idea how we can protect ourselves. We'll get Mr. Archer's permission in writing first. We'll get him to sign a statement saying that we're to be in charge of Horse until he can take over. Then nobody could accuse us of stealing."

That seemed legal enough. I wasn't prepared to go to reform school, not even for Horse, but it still seemed to me that my brothers were getting carried away by their own wishful thinking.

"Have you forgotten Mr. Archer's in hospital?" I reminded them. "How's he supposed to sign a statement?"

"We can hitchhike over to Kitchener tomorrow and go see him at the hospital. Gran won't mind if we all go together. Then, when we've got the signed statement from Mr. Archer, we'll just hide Horse, and that's that."

I was way behind them, as usual. "Hey, wait a minute," I said. "If we got a signed statement from Mr. Archer putting us in charge, why do we have to hide Horse?"

Julian and Maxwell regarded me pityingly. They had less innocence than I had. "Because we don't trust Mr. Crossley," Julian said. "We can't guard Horse all the time, and he'd just go sell her behind our backs, I bet, like he's doing behind Mr. Archer's. Even if we sued him, the grown-ups would all be on his side. Look at Grandma. You'd have thought she'd have been on our side, but she wasn't," he finished bitterly.

It all seemed utterly complicated to me, but then Maxwell and Julian have a way of complicating the simplest things, so that you need several degrees and an IQ of 500 to sort them out. It was sometimes easier to accept the idea that

34

they knew what they were talking about. I was feeling pretty sour about grown-ups myself at that moment. They were always so righteous in everything they did and, no matter what Grandma might say, I couldn't see that Mr. Crossley had any right to dispose of Mr. Archer's possessions so offhandedly, as though the poor old man had no say in the matter at all.

"Well—just say that I agree with you," I said tentatively. "Where were you thinking of hiding Horse? Grandma wouldn't let us have her here, because she's on Mr. Crossley's side, so that's out."

Julian and Maxwell looked sheepish. With a slight simper, Maxwell said, "We thought you might know somewhere."

"Oh," I said tartly. "Well, thanks very much! I don't think much of a plan that fizzles out at the most important part. I thought you had it all worked out."

"Well, if that's the way you feel, don't bother," said Julian indignantly. "We just thought three brains were better than two, that's all."

They were cunning. They knew if they decided to leave me out, I would want to be included. Besides, it would give me great pleasure to keep Horse from Mr. Crossley's clutches, and maybe save Mr. Archer's old house at the same time. Then I realized that something strange had happened to me. The thought of the old house no longer depressed me. It had become somebody's home, a warm, living place that somebody loved. It broke my heart to think of Mr. Archer being forced to give it up, just because he was old and no match for the wiles of someone like Mr. Crossley. I took a deep breath and committed myself.

"Well, there is a fenced property near our school," I said. "It's rented by a farmer, but he doesn't put his cattle in there until later on when his own pasture gets thin. There's a pond in it, too, and it's secluded. I suppose we could leave Horse there for a while until we think of somewhere better."

Julian let out a whoop of delight. "I know that field! Why didn't I think of that? Oh, Jo, that would be great! It's far enough away so Mr. Crossley wouldn't think of looking there. We'll leave her gate open so he'll think she's wandered away by herself. He can't spend all his time looking for her. It's not like he lives here. He'll have to give up after a while and Horse will be safe. Oh, Jo, that's great!"

He and Maxwell collapsed on the bed in gales of laughter, at the thought of outwitting Mr. Crossley. "When the coast's clear," Julian said, serious again, "we can take our time making other arrangements for Horse. Maybe we can board her out cheap somewhere."

I knew they were dreaming. Stables were way beyond our reach, but right now they were so exhilarated they could see no obstacles ahead of them that could not be surmounted when the time came.

Julian sat upright, rubbing his hands purposefully. "So this is what we'll do. Tomorrow we'll go and see Mr. Archer—right? Then on Friday I'll take my bike to school, but I'll come home on the bus. Grandma won't notice. Then when we're supposed to be over at Mr. Archer's in the evening, I'll ride Horse over to the field, pick up my bike at school and cycle home." Our two schools happened to be less than a quarter of a mile apart, which did simplify matters a great deal. "Everything's going to work out just great, you see!"

I had to believe him, because I was committed too far now to back out, but I still wondered whether my head needed seeing to.

"We ought to prick our fingers and mingle our blood

36

and swear that we'll die before we let Horse fall into Mr. Crossley's clutches," proclaimed Maxwell with gory relish; but this was too bloodthirsty for Julian and me, so we settled on solemnly shaking hands to seal our partnership in intrigue. Then they went off to compose the statement to take to Mr. Archer.

Sitting back on the bed, I felt limp and slightly unreal. I had wanted something to happen, and all of a sudden things were happening with a vengeance. I didn't know whether to be scared or excited, so I settled on a bit of both and decided to become a fatalist. With two brothers like Julian and Maxwell, it was the only way to retain your sanity.

A Visit with Mr. Archer

· 4 ·

Next morning we informed Grandma that we intended to visit Mr. Archer after lunch. She thought it was a good idea and commended us for being so thoughtful. Even when we told her we were going to hitchhike she raised no objections. I suppose she thought that anyone who intended to kidnap Maxwell and Julian would soon return them after a couple of days. They might even pay Grandma to take them back.

Margaret had a boyfriend who was coming up from Toronto that afternoon to see her. His name was Wallace Pindlebury, and he was a student at the art college. He had silky golden hair and a wispy ginger mustache. I always thought he looked like the "before" picture in a body-building advertisement, but Margaret thought he looked romantic. While she was primping upstairs, it occurred to me that Wallace would probably be driving her into Kitchener and could take us, too. I went upstairs and asked her.

"Oh, Jo," she said, with a pained expression, "I haven't seen him for three months. If he feels I'm using him to chauffeur my family around, I'll probably never see him again."

"Exactly. I thought I was doing you a good turn," I said. But she didn't appreciate my thoughtfulness. We ended up on the road thumbing a ride.

We didn't have to wait long before we got a lift in a yellow Land Rover. The driver was an older man, large and brusque and tweedy, with twinkling eyes. "I know who you are," he said. "You're Mrs. Tate's grandchildren. Which one of you fell off the horse the other day?"

So this was John's grandfather. I felt nervously excited to think they had talked about me. "It was me," I said, giving him my best smile. "I'm fine now."

"That's the spirit," he told me. "A good rider has to take a few tumbles in his stride. Do you like riding?"

"Oh, yes," I said. "I love horses." I was keeping my fingers crossed, desperately hoping that Maxwell and Julian wouldn't come up with some stupid, tactless remark. After all, I'd only been riding for a week. However, for once, they remained silent. Either they were overawed by the presence of Mr. Holmes, or were so wrapped up in their errand, they hadn't thought to spare for anything else.

"You must come over sometime and have a look around our stables," invited Mr. Holmes.

"I'd love to," I said shyly.

"Well, trot over any time. There's always someone there to show you around. Just tell them I said it was okay."

I thanked him, feeling my spirits lift. Perhaps I would see John again after all. It must have been a lucky providence that had sent old Mr. Holmes to give us a ride. As Grandma had said, he seemed awfully nice, and I liked him a lot better than John's father. He dropped us off right outside the hospital and said, "Don't forget now. Any time you feel like it, just pop over."

Julian and Maxwell were impressed. "He likes us," declared Maxwell, which I thought was a bit conceited of him, since I had done all the talking. "When shall we go? Tonight?"

"Look!" I said sternly. "Let's do one thing at a time, shall we? Have you got that declaration ready for Mr. Archer to sign? We don't want to fumble anything at the last minute."

Standing on the hospital steps, surrounded by Sunday afternoon visitors, we gave the paper a final checking over. They had spent a lot of thought on it, printing it neatly on white bond paper after I had corrected the spelling and grammar. It really looked quite professional. Maxwell read it through slowly:

I, MR. ERNEST ARCHER, THE UNDERSIGNED, being of sound mind, do hereby bequeath my horse named HORSE into the care and protection of JOANNA, JULIAN AND MAXWELL LONGFELLOW to look after to the best of their ability until such time as my health has improved enough for me to take said HORSE back into my own custody, or otherwise dispose of her future in any manner of which I see fit to approve.

There were dotted lines for all our signatures, and the date was written out in full. The wording seemed a bit clumsy to me, but Julian informed me with authority that all legal documents took the long way around to say anything, and I had to admit it looked impressive.

"Okay," I said, putting it in my pocket, "let's go and find out what floor he's on."

I went to the desk and asked the receptionist. She looked

up the information in a card index and gave it to me, but as we headed for the elevators she called me back. "I'm sorry, no children allowed in the wards. They can stay here. I'll keep an eye on them."

We stared at her dumbfounded. I shepherded Julian and Maxwell out of earshot behind a potted palm and exploded. "Now what? You and your crazy plans! You said you'd thought of everything. If I go up there alone, Mr. Archer isn't going to sign away his horse to me. He doesn't know me from Adam! He'd have me thrown out!"

"No he wouldn't, not if you told him you're our sister."

"I will not!" I announced firmly. "I will not expose myself to further ridicule! The whole thing is stupid anyway. I knew it was! I think we should go home."

Julian and Maxwell looked shocked. I might have said something indecent. Leaving me out in the cold, they went into a huddle. After a moment of fretting and fuming on my part, Julian said that he was going to go up to the receptionist and ask where the washroom was. "And while I'm talking to her," he told me, "you and Max make a dash for the elevators. Okay?"

"No!" I cried. "Absolutely not! I won't. . . ." But Julian was already halfway across to the desk, and Maxwell was sidling along the wall behind the potted plants. With a final dash he made it inside an elevator going up. Out of the corner of my eye I saw Julian chatting amiably with the girl behind the desk. I had no choice but to follow Maxwell, since I had the declaration in my pocket. Squeezing in, just as the doors slid shut, I squashed Maxwell against the back wall to make him as unobtrusive as possible. I hoped that anybody who saw him would think he was a patient. He certainly sounded like one. He was having difficulty breathing with my shoulder in his mouth. As soon as we got off, he started complaining loudly, until I told him very firmly to shut up or I'd walk off and leave him. There were a couple of nurses on duty up here, too, but they were busy talking to each other. Mingling with the flow of visitors, we managed to scurry past unseen.

A new thought then occurred to me. Suppose Mr. Archer already had visitors, maybe even Mr. Crossley and his wife. I stopped dead. Maxwell, bumping headlong into me, said peevishly, "What's up now?"

"What if Mr. Crossley's visiting Mr. Archer?" I said in a hollow voice.

Maxwell shrugged. "So what? We'll get rid of him. We'll tell him the hospital's on fire." I couldn't protest anymore. By this time my mind was just not functioning properly.

We checked the room numbers until we found the right one. Maxwell peeped in and beckoned to me excitedly. "He's there and he's alone! He looks like he's asleep."

I peered over Maxwell's shoulder and saw that there were three other patients in the room and they all had visitors, but Mr. Archer's bed was separated by a half-drawn curtain. Looking anxiously up and down the corridor, I handed the paper and a pen to Maxwell. "Get him to sign it before he does anything else, before you even talk to him!" I ordered. "I'll stay here and keep watch. Hurry now!"

Maxwell bounded into the ward, and I heard him hissing loudly in Mr. Archer's ear, "Mr. Archer, wake up, wake up! It's me, Maxwell Longfellow. If you value Horse's life, sign this right away and don't ask questions!"

I groaned inwardly, wishing that Maxwell could be a little less theatrical at times. By now I was feeling like one of the chief characters in an international spy plot. I only hoped

42

the other people in the ward didn't know the rule about no children allowed.

The corridor was reassuringly empty, but just as I was relaxing, a tea trolley, pushed by two nursing aides, turned the corner and came heading straight toward me. I ducked my head around the door to warn Maxwell. He had managed to wake Mr. Archer, who didn't seem to be able to grasp what was going on. That was quite understandable. Maxwell had forced the pen into his hand and was urging him in a hoarse voice to sign.

"Sign what?" asked Mr. Archer in a dazed voice. He was a chubby little man, with a fringe of white hair. He seemed just the sort of person who would own a horse like Horse. Slipping around to the other side of the bed, I whispered urgently:

"Mr. Archer, we're not supposed to be here, but please trust us. We want you to sign this paper giving us full charge of Horse until you're better, because we're afraid someone might try to sell her. If we have your signature on this, we'll take good care of her—cross my heart—but please hurry. Please trust us!"

He was still sedated, but my urgency and the mention of Horse must have gotten through to him. Maxwell steadied the paper and I guided Mr. Archer's hand and we got his somewhat shaky signature in the proper place. He struggled up to a sitting position and seemed to be trying to clear the fogginess in his brain. "Is Horse all right?" he asked anxiously.

"Horse is just fine!" I assured him. I eased him down again and covered him up. "She's just waiting for you to get better and come home. Now don't you worry about a thing. We're going to take care of everything."

He closed his eyes, and I noticed he was smiling. I felt a warm sort of a feeling that we were saving Horse for him. I beckoned to Maxwell and stuffed the signed declaration back into my pocket. Tiptoeing out, we bumped squarely into the tea trolley coming in. The woman in charge took one look at Maxwell and said, "What are you doing here, sonny?" She eyed me with disapproval. "Don't you know you're not allowed to bring children into the wards?" Regarding me closer, she said suspiciously, "How old are you, anyway?"

"Eighteen," I lied. I wasn't sure what the age limit was.

"And I'm twenty-one," said Maxwell in his most superior voice. "I happen to be a midget, and I don't like being called sonny!"

She goggled at him, and for a moment I believe she was almost fooled. I wasn't about to find out. I seized him by the neck of his sweater and fled down the corridor to the elevators. Downstairs we picked up Julian and got out of there as fast as we could. We had covered two blocks before we felt it was safe to slow down.

"We got it!" exclaimed Maxwell, whooping joyously. "Now we're in business!"

Walking triumphantly back to the highway to get a lift, what should we see parked outside a restaurant in a small shopping area, but Wallace Pindlebury's Volkswagen? There was only one like it in the world. It was painted a luminous shocking pink, stenciled with multihued daisies, and bore the inspiring motto, THINK BEAUTIFUL, on both sides. The car was too much of a temptation to pass by. We sat down beside it on the curb waiting for Margaret and Wallace to come out of the restaurant.

Margaret spied us first and looked sick. She would have ignored us, but we all sang out in prearranged harmony, "Fancy seeing you here! What a coincidence!"

44

"I bet," she murmured under her breath.

"I think your car is beautiful, Wallace," I said, batting my eyelids at him. "I've always wanted to ride in it."

He eyed us helplessly, his wispy mustache twitching. "I suppose that means you want a ride home," he said with noticeable lack of enthusiasm.

Before the words were out of his mouth, the three of us had squeezed into the back seat of the car. Scowling, Margaret got into the front. I leaned over the seat and said sweetly, "I think it's so nice that Wallace thinks beautiful just like his motto says, Margaret. Some people would have just left us sitting on the curb and not cared at all."

Wallace and Margaret were silent all the way home. I could tell by his expression that he could hardly wait to rush back to Toronto and get his car painted solid black. I didn't care. We had Mr. Archer's signed declaration, I had made friends with John's grandfather, and now we had a lift right to the front door. It was one of those days when nothing could go wrong!

Our Plan Is Upset

· 5 ·

My smug feeling didn't last long. On Tuesday Maxwell came down with a nice case of German measles. Julian and I had had them before, so we weren't too worried, but Maxwell was furious. He took it as a personal affront that a germ should dare to attack him at such a time. I felt sorry for Grandma, who had to nurse him.

Then, on Thursday, Julian came home with a sore throat. He kept it to himself and only told me when I came upstairs to bed.

"I couldn't have German measles twice, could I, Jo?" he asked anxiously.

"Of course not!" I told him with finality. "Nobody does!" I took his temperature. He had a slight fever, and I began to get worried. "You can't have it!" I declared in desperation. "You must absolutely tell yourself not to have it!"

46

He looked at me sadly. "My back feels itchy like I'm going to get spots."

"Oh Julian, no!" I sat down on the bed in despair. "What are we going to do, then?"

Julian shrugged. "I don't feel that bad. So long as the spots don't start showing, I'm all right. If I can just hang on until tomorrow night, Horse will be safe—then it won't matter."

I knew I ought to have reasoned with him, but I couldn't. Without him, all our planning and scheming would come to nothing. We went to bed keeping our fingers crossed.

In the morning he looked a bit flushed but told me he felt all right. He left first on his bicycle, and Margaret and I followed on the school bus. Halfway to school the bus stopped suddenly, and I peered out of the window to see what was holding us up. I saw Julian sitting in the ditch amid the ruins of his bicycle. Margaret had seen him, too. We almost fell over each other trying to get out first.

"Julian!" I cried. "What happened?"

He looked dazed. "I felt dizzy," he said in a small voice. "I think I've ruined my bicycle."

Margaret, who could be relied upon to become hysterical in emergencies, started screeching for an ambulance, but the bus driver was more practical. He asked the driver of a truck that had drawn up behind the bus to take Julian and the ruined bicycle back home. We watched him go and got back in the bus. I thought the school day would never end. I couldn't concentrate on anything. My only thought was that it was now up to me to save Horse, and I didn't feel capable of it. I felt so rotten, I almost hoped I was coming down with German measles myself.

As soon as we got home, Margaret and I went upstairs

to see how the boys were. They were propped up in bed scowling at each other, one white and one spotted. I'd never seen a more depressed-looking pair.

"Well," said Margaret brightly, "welcome to Disneyland!"

"Oh, buzz off!" Julian told her.

"Well, thanks a lot," said Margaret. "I just came up to comfort the sick, but if the sick don't want to be comforted I'm sure I can find plenty of other things to do."

She marched off in a huff, and I said to Julian, "What now?"

"You'll have to do it, Jo," he said solemnly.

I bit my lip. I had been expecting him to say that all along. "I don't know whether I can!" I said beseechingly. "I mean I've only been riding one week, and only in the field. I've never been out on the road. Suppose traffic makes Horse nervous. If she bolted, I couldn't control her. I'd fall off for sure, and Horse would run away. Then where would we be?"

"No worse off than we are now," groaned Maxwell.

"Except that I might be mutilated for life," I said, but that aspect of it didn't seem to worry them. "Trust you to be the only person in the world to get German measles twice, Julian."

Julian was offended. "Gran said Mother had it twice, too, so you see it runs in the family. It's not my fault."

"Anyway, he's got a plan," said Maxwell smugly. "You can get up very early tomorrow morning, about half-past four, and go before anybody's up. There won't be any traffic about so early. We figured you might not want to ride in traffic, and we didn't want anything to happen to Horse."

"Well, thanks very much," I said haughtily.

"But it would be better, Jo," Julian said eagerly. "If I

were you, I'd go over and get Horse tonight, after supper, and leave her in the next field. It's empty. You can put the tack in our barn, too, then you'll be all ready to go first thing in the morning."

"You mean leave her in Mr. Holmes's field?"

"Sure, why not? If you wait until it's almost dark to bring her over, no one will see her, and you'll be gone in the morning before anyone's up."

I had to agree that there was something to be said for their reasoning. It would be better for Horse, too, because there would be less chance of anyone spotting us.

"But when I've left her at the field, how do I get back?" I said. "It'll take about an hour to ride there, but if I have to walk back I won't be home for hours and hours, and Gran's sure to miss me. What am I going to tell her?"

Then Julian produced his *coup de grâce*. Fishing under his pillow, he produced the ten-dollar bill that Mr. Crossley had given us. "Get yourself a taxi," he said expansively, handing it over to me. "There's a telephone booth on the corner by your school. You see, I told you we could use the money!"

I had to admit a grudging admiration for these brothers of mine. Nothing seemed to faze them. I felt sure they would go far in the world, but whether the world would be the better or worse for it was another matter.

Anyway, after supper I told Grandma that I was going to tuck Horse up for the night, and off I went to Mr. Archer's place. I was quite excited now about the morning. Riding Horse that distance all by myself, along the road, too, would be a great step forward in my riding career. She came to meet me with her usual greeting, and went through all my pockets. Then I rode her, getting some practice in until the sun was a great red ball sinking behind the skeleton arms of the trees. Then I led her out of the field and down the path, making sure I left her gate open to put Mr. Crossley off the scent.

She followed me like a lamb, only butting me once or twice impatiently, when I was slow in getting the gate unwired into the Holmes's property. It was not used much, and it was rusted. By the time we reached the field next to our house, the moon was already climbing palely into the sky. I unsaddled her and put on her halter, then gave her a little pat on her rump. "Off you go," I said. "And don't draw attention to yourself."

She came with me to the fence and watched me go into the house. I went straight up to bed and slept like a log. Julian had put the alarm under his pillow so that it wouldn't wake anyone else. He tiptoed in and woke me, giving me the good luck sign.

"Remember, it's up to you now, Jo," he whispered.

It was strange being up so early in a silent house. I took some milk and cookies on my way out, stepping over Butch on the doormat. He thumped his tail but couldn't be bothered to get up. The morning smelled of grass and lilacs, and the birds and the frogs were singing in chorus. I had never realized that early morning was such a noisy time.

I couldn't see Horse, so I fetched the tack, and went up the field calling softly to her. At the top of the hill, there she was below me, and I nearly died of shock! She was no longer alone! There was a handsome gray stallion with her, and they were romping and whickering around the far end of the field like a couple of puppies. My heart immediately sank like a stone. I was positive there had been no other horse in the field last night. I put the saddle down and took off after her, but I was a poor substitute for her gorgeous new boyfriend. She ignored me completely, no matter how I begged and appealed to her. The three of us raced around and around the field, with me getting redder in the face and more breathless by the minute, until, of course, disaster struck again. I caught my foot in a groundhog hole and sprawled full-length on the ground. I felt a sharp pain run up my leg where I had hurt it before.

"Oh, no!" I wailed. "Oh, no!" If I couldn't catch Horse on two sound legs, what chance had I now? Frustrated and helpless, I buried my face in the grass and burst into tears. But crying like a baby wasn't going to help me. My self-pity gave way to fury. We were doing our utmost to save Horse, and she didn't appreciate our efforts one bit. I had one good leg left and, resolved to fight to the finish, I hauled myself up prepared to try again. Then, to make my morning complete, who should I see looking down at me from the top of the hill but John Holmes on Queenie?

He rode down the slope, and I could tell by his face that he was none too pleased by what he saw. "Is that your horse?" he asked.

I had to vent my frustration on someone. "Yes it is!" I flung back at him. "And I can't catch her because of that dumb, stupid stallion! What's it doing here, anyway? It wasn't here last night. Now I've hurt my leg again, and I don't know what to do!"

Without a word, he turned Queenie around and opened the gate into the adjoining field. Then he galloped after the stallion, gave it a good slap on its rear and sent it scurrying through the gate. With the light of her life gone, Horse came to me at once, whinnying gently, and nosing in my pockets for sugar.

"Traitor!" I hissed at her, but I made sure I had a firm hold on her halter this time.

John rode back to me and dismounted. "That dumb,

51

stupid stallion happens to be our prize stud," he informed me. "He wasn't in this field last night, but he can jump fences when he has a reason to. What was your horse doing here, anyway?"

"I left her here," I said, sniffing. I couldn't bear to be cross-examined after all I had just been through.

"No need to start crying," said John curtly, so of course I started to cry harder. In the end, he couldn't stand it, and gave me his handkerchief. I was so susceptible to this small act of kindness that, before I could stop myself, I blurted out everything to him. I figured our plan was ruined now, anyway, because I couldn't ride Horse with my bad leg. I don't know what I expected of him, but I certainly didn't think he would laugh, which he did. He laughed so hard I became resentful.

"I don't see that it's so funny," I said.

"Don't you?" He pulled himself together, but his mouth still twitched. "Maybe I have a peculiar sense of humor. So you want to abduct this horse, do you? Well, I'm on your side. I think I would, too."

"You—you would?" I gasped, gaping at him like a moron.

"Certainly. If someone tried to sell my horse without asking me I'd be furious. There's an old barn on the far side of our property that isn't used anymore. You could keep her there for a few days if you like and nobody'd be any the wiser. I have to go back on Monday, of course, but you could let Jim in on your secret. He's a good sort. You wouldn't have to worry about him."

I was incapable of speech. I thought I must be dreaming. Problems just didn't solve themselves as easily as this, particularly when I seemed to have messed everything up from the start. There had to be a catch somewhere, because it was too perfect to be true. At Holmwood Farms Horse would be safe, for who would ever suspect such an elegant establishment of abducting a small, slightly overweight Quarter horse with a tendency to lean on people?

"Wouldn't your father, or your grandfather find out?" I suggested timidly.

"Well, they might if they were here, but luckily they flew down to Florida for a few days, so they won't be here this weekend. Of course she couldn't stay indefinitely, but leave it to me. I might fix up something. I have a friend at college whose parents have a place a few miles from here, and they board horses as a sideline. If you'd be interested, I could probably get you cheap rates."

"Could you?" I swallowed hard and asked, "How cheap is cheap?"

John laughed. "Well, their regular rates I believe are sixteen dollars a week." Noticing my dismay, he continued quickly, "But I wouldn't expect you to pay that. Another guy at college boarded his horse there once when they were moving, and I seem to remember he only got charged half-price. I expect they'd do the same for me. I could find out."

My mind was busy calculating sums at a furious rate. Half of sixteen dollars was eight dollars, and between us, as pocket money, Julian, Maxwell and I made four dollars a week. I suppose to someone like John Holmes, eight dollars a week was a real bargain, and I was afraid he would lose interest if I told him how we were financially situated. While I wavered, Horse nibbled my neck affectionately, and that decided me. Surely three able young people could find some way to earn an extra four dollars a week. After all, it wasn't a fortune. John was waiting for my answer while Queenie and Horse eyed each other warily over our heads.

I took a deep breath and said shyly, "That would be awfully nice of you. I sure would appreciate it."

"That's all right." He gave me a warm smile and seemed to be enjoying our little conspiracy. "I only hope we don't end up in jail together." I could hardly believe he was the same person who had treated me so casually the first day I had met him. He was looking at Horse, and I wondered what he was thinking. She looked decidedly rakish beside the elegant Queenie, but all he said was, "If I give you a leg up, do you think you could ride her? We ought to get her hidden away as soon as possible, don't you think?"

I agreed heartily. He saddled Horse for me and helped me up and, except for an occasional twinge in my leg, I managed very well. With the sun coming up behind us we rode down past the sleeping stables and the empty paddocks. Being the only ones up created a sort of bond between us, and I wasn't so shy of him anymore.

"I don't know what I would have done without you," I confessed in a moment of gratitude.

He grinned at me. "Forget it. It's nice to have something to break the monotony around here."

I thought he was kidding me and I said so, but he was serious.

"You don't know what it's like," he said, his voice suddenly hard. "I can never ride for pleasure, unless I get up early in the morning like this. The rest of the day it's just training, training, training from morning to night. Sometimes I dream I'm smothering in gold medals, silver cups and red ribbons. You don't know what it's like. You should try it some time, and see if you like it!"

How could he not know how lucky he was? How could he be so ungrateful? I would have given ten years of my life to have had one quarter of what he had, but I didn't dare risk

54

his displeasure by telling him so. After his little outburst he had become quiet, and his face looked sullen. We finished the rest of the ride in silence.

The old barn stood by itself in a grove of trees and was part of the original homestead. It was an ideal place to hide Horse. We put her in a stall, and John said he would get Jim to bring her bedding and feed. Then he said, if I wanted to talk with Horse for a while, he would fetch his car around and take me home. He had a racy little foreign model that made Wallace's Volkswagen look sick. I only wished Margaret could have seen me.

"How long have you been riding?" he asked me on the way home.

I bit my lip. I was on the point of lying to him, but friendship couldn't be based on lies. "Just one week," I mumbled.

"One *week!*" He stared at me and nearly swerved the little car into the ditch. Then he started to laugh again. "I thought you were an expert!" he exploded. "One week! Oh, you're kidding!" He couldn't seem to get over it. I sat hunched up and miserable beside him, until he noticed how quiet I was. Then he reached over and patted my hand. "Cheer up. I'll probably be here next week on Thursday because there's an important show coming up soon. I should have some news for you by then. Why don't you come over for supper and bring your brothers if they're better? I'd rather like to meet them."

I didn't tell him he'd be sorry. I thanked him and said I'd love to, and by that time we were at our house. As he opened the door for me, he said, "Oh, by the way, what's your horse's name?"

With crimson cheeks I mumbled, "You're not going to believe this, but she's called Horse."

"I beg your pardon."

"Horse," I said. "H-O-R-S-E."

"You're right," he said, "I don't believe it!" And then we were laughing together like old friends, and it was wonderful.

Mr. Crossley Is Outwitted

· 6 ·

When I got back to my room, I sneaked into the sun porch to tell Maxwell and Julian what had happened. For once in my life I had the pleasure of seeing them regard me with something like respect, but they weren't so optimistic about the extra four dollars we had to find.

"It would be easy if we were in the city," said Julian despondently. "We could wash cars and cut lawns and baby-sit, but nobody does those things on farms, at least I don't think they do."

"Well, I told John to go ahead and arrange it, so we've got to do something," I told them firmly. "Think!"

We all thought, screwing our faces up into horrible contortions, but nobody came up with any bright ideas.

"Perhaps they'd let us board Horse for four dollars and let us work off the rest," suggested Julian. "We could go after school. Mr. Archer told us it was hard to get good stable help. He said he was lucky to get us."

"How much did he pay you?"

"Nothing, but he would have, if he could have afforded it."

That didn't seem to help our problem. I was becoming a bit weary of problems. As soon as one was solved, another cropped up.

"I think Julian's got a good idea," said Maxwell loyally. "We work hard and people can trust us. We'd be a real bargain at four dollars a week. I bet they'd snap us up."

I decided to let that pass. I had missed a lot of sleep, and I was beginning to feel tired. "Well," I said, "we'll just have to look in the weekly paper and, if there isn't anything, I guess that's all we can do." I didn't relish the idea of explaining to John, but by this time, probably nothing we did would surprise him. I went back to bed and fell into a deep sleep, and when I woke up Grandma was peering down at me anxiously.

"Aren't you getting up, Joanna? It's nearly ten o'clock. Don't tell me *you're* getting German measles again."

"I expect I am," I said wickedly, making round eyes at her over the sheet. "It must be a peculiarity of our family."

"Oh, dear!" sighed Grandma. "One thing after another." She took the boys' breakfast tray downstairs and came back with a thermometer to stick under my tongue. Of course my temperature was normal, but even when I told her I had been kidding, she didn't seem convinced.

"I've never known you to stay in bed this late before. Perhaps it's just developing. You'd better not get up this morning. I'll bring you up some breakfast."

I didn't bother to argue anymore. I felt I could use a little pampering after my harrowing morning. Margaret

brought my breakfast up on a tray and said, "You're a phor
Jo. There's nothing wrong with you. You just want to ge
out of your share of housecleaning."

"You don't have any compassion, Margaret," I said,
between mouthfuls of puffed wheat. "Why don't you think
beautiful, like Wallace Pindlebury?"

She stalked out of the room in disgust, and Julian and
Maxwell came in to help themselves to my toast and jam. We
were discussing our future plans for Horse, when a knock on
the front door silenced us. Maxwell scurried into the front
bedroom and returned in a hurry. "It's him," he announced
in a hollow voice. "It's Mr. Crossley. Let's get back into bed
quick!"

I pulled the covers over my head, my heart thumping. I
hadn't expected a confrontation this soon. I hoped that
Grandma would be able to head him off, but soon there were
footsteps on the stairs and Grandma opened the door quietly.

"Are you awake, Joanna? Mr. Crossley thinks you left
the gate of Horse's field open last night, and now she's gone.
Have you any idea where she'd be?"

I didn't want to tell any more lies than I absolutely had
to, so I gave a plausible imitation of a dying groan, which
could have meant anything.

"I know you wouldn't do it purposely, dear, but maybe
if you weren't feeling well last night you weren't as careful as
usual. Nobody's blaming you, but Mr. Crossley does want to
find Horse."

He certainly did. He had come up the stairs after
Grandma, and I saw his florid face peering over her shoulder.
"I've got the trailer waiting," he said in exasperation, "and
now there's no horse, after I've gone to all the trouble and
expense of renting it. I'm sorry if you're sick, but you've got
to understand that I did expect you to take a bit more trouble

than this after I paid you. Have you any idea where the horse could have gone? Has it ever got out before?"

He was making me mad, calling Horse an "it." Forgetting that I was supposed to be dying, I scowled at him. "I don't know. Why don't you ask Mr. Archer, or don't you want him to know you're selling Horse behind his back?"

He didn't like that at all. He pushed past Grandma to the foot of my bed. "Now look here, my girl, there are some things that don't concern you! You were paid to look after it, that's all. I've gone to a lot of trouble finding a home for it, and I don't have the time to go running around the countryside looking for it. I'm a busy man!"

I should have kept my mouth shut and not provoked him. Grandma was trying to soothe him, and I was afraid I might have made him suspicious. Swallowing my pride, I thought I had better apologize. Making my voice sound weak, as though I were not long for this world, I said, "I'm sorry, Mr. Crossley. I shouldn't have said that, but we did take good care of Horse. Maybe she opened the gate herself. She's quite smart, you know. Why don't you take a drive around and see if you can see her? She can't have gone far."

Mr. Crossley was trying to curb his temper, but I could see he was ready to explode. "One horse looks just like another to me! Someone could have stolen it for all I know. Do you expect me to call on every farmer for miles around to see if they have a horse that doesn't belong to them? Oh, really, this is too exasperating!"

Grandma made sympathetic noises. "I don't think anyone around here would steal a horse. They're mostly Mennonites and they're very good people, Mr. Crossley. It's too bad the children are sick, or they could have driven around with you. They're so fond of Horse. I do hope she

60

turns up. They were most upset when they heard she was going to be sold."

I groaned inwardly, willing Grandma to be quiet. I didn't like the way Mr. Crossley was looking at me, and I knew I had to get rid of him quickly. Sitting up in bed, I announced purposefully, "Grandma, I think I'm going to be sick!"

"Oh, dear!" Grandma literally pushed Mr. Crossley out of the room, at the same time urging me to run to the bathroom. She couldn't just abandon Mr. Crossley and, by the time she had seen him out, and come back upstairs, I was sitting on the bed, giggling my head off.

"I thought you were feeling ill," she said suspiciously.

"I've just had one of those miraculous cures you read about," I told her. "I don't think I've got German measles at all."

She shook her head wearily. "You children are too much for me at times. I wish your father would settle down like a normal man and take you off my hands. Now what can have happened to Horse?"

"I wouldn't worry too much about her, Grandma," I said reassuringly. "She's a pretty smart horse. She knows how to take care of herself."

"Well, that poor man is pretty upset, and I can't say I blame him. I've promised to phone around to see if anyone's seen her, and if she turns up I've got his phone number. That's all I can do. At least he says he's going to keep the news from Mr. Archer until he's better, which is something. I wouldn't want him worrying, too."

I said nothing, and Grandma, no doubt thinking that I was fretting about Horse, dropped the subject. As the days went by and no word came of Horse's whereabouts,

Grandma gradually became resigned to the fact that Horse had found herself another home, which suited Julian, Maxwell and me just fine.

Thursday came around, the day of our visit to Holmwood Farms. We had told Grandma about Mr. Holmes's invitation to come over to the stables whenever we felt like it, and that's where she thought we were going now. She didn't know about John. That would have taken too much explaining.

"I don't understand you, Joanna," she said to me. "You wear slacks to school, then put on your prettiest dress to go around the stables. Sometimes I think you're all upside down."

She didn't make me change, though, and secretly, I think, she was fostering the hope that I was turning into a lady, at last.

My two previous visits to Holmwood Farms had been confined to the barns and stables. Now, walking up the elegant driveway, flanked by Maxwell and Julian, I was overpowered by the luxury of the house and gardens. Suddenly I felt panicky. The three of us didn't seem to belong here at all. Even my best dress didn't help. I felt like sneaking home again, but Maxwell and Julian had no such qualms. They marched ahead of me up the steps and banged on the brass knocker. Then they discovered a bell and had a go at that, while I cringed in shame, wishing I didn't have to be associated with them.

We were let in by a housekeeper, who seemed to be expecting us. She led us through a paneled hall and down a couple of steps into a sunken living room. One wall was completely taken up by a stone fireplace, and there were three bouncy velvet chesterfields, bright blue with orange cushions. A brass bowl of yellow tulips stood in the bay window. There was a rich fragrance in the room, which might have been the flowers or the logs burning in the fireplace, but to me it was the smell of opulence. Grandma's house never smelled like that.

John was out in the barn and, while the housekeeper went to fetch him, we sat stiffly, like three wooden statues, on the chesterfield in front of the fire. I was wondering how you could tell anyone who lived in a house like this that it was impossible to raise eight dollars a week. Then John came running down the steps to welcome us, and all I could remember was how we had laughed together when I told him Horse was called Horse.

"Well," he said, "you made it! That's great! I've got good news for you. They've agreed to take Horse, and I even managed to knock them down a couple of dollars on one condition—that you boys go over there a couple of nights a week to help clean out the stables. Otherwise I'm afraid it would be ten. I didn't think you'd mind, because you'd probably be going over to see Horse anyway."

I could see he was feeling quite pleased with himself and expecting us to be, too. We must have disappointed him badly. He looked at our blank faces and said, puzzled, "Well? Did I do something wrong?"

"Oh, no—no. . . ." My face was scarlet like my dress. "It's just. . . ." I bit my lip, wishing that I was a hundred miles away. "It's just that we don't have six dollars."

"You what?" His face registered blank dismay. "But I thought you said you could afford eight! I thought I was doing you a good turn beating them down to six."

I had to confess everything then because Maxwell and Julian, cowards that they were, had lost their tongues and were cringing behind me. When I had finished, miserable with shame, John said nothing. He turned away and made a great show of poking the fire. Then I noticed his shoulders shaking, and I knew he was laughing again, or trying very hard not to. I was getting rather tired of being an object of ridicule. I wanted to be liked because of myself, not because I was one long continuous joke.

At last he turned back to us and said, "You're fantastic, you know that? You really are."

The way he said it, I didn't take it as a compliment. "I'm sorry," I mumbled. "But I really did think we could raise four dollars, I really did. It didn't seem so much then, and all I was worried about was finding a place to keep Horse." My voice trailed away in despair. We only had to find two dollars now, but when you don't have it, two dollars might as well be a hundred.

"I see." John was still having trouble keeping a straight face. "Well, suppose I make up the extra two dollars a week for you?"

"No!" I said it so forcibly, he was startled. The last thing I wanted from him was charity. I didn't want him to feel that he was obliged to be friends with me because he was giving us money. I would rather never see him again.

It seemed we had reached an impasse. We stood looking helplessly at each other. I don't know how Julian and Maxwell were feeling, but I felt about two inches tall.

John pursed his lips together and frowned. "Okay, Joanna," he said slowly, "seeing that the boys will be working at my friend's place, why don't you come and work here on Saturday mornings? Jim can always use more help. I'll ask my grandfather tomorrow, if you like, but I'm sure he'll say yes. You've met him, haven't you?"

I nodded, relief making me temporarily speechless. "Oh, that would be wonderful!" I said at last. "It would solve everything. I'd really work hard. I'd do anything they wanted me to."

"You don't have to break your back for two dollars," John said, his eyes laughing at me. "Come over on Saturday morning and see my grandfather. I'll tell him to expect you."

So another problem was settled, and we could relax. The housekeeper brought us a jug of fruit punch and a plateful of pastries and waited on us as though we were important people, and we really began to enjoy ourselves. At some time during the evening, when Maxwell and Julian were regaling us with tales of the time they had worked for Mr. Archer, John said, "You really think a lot of him and Horse, don't you?"

"It's not only that," I said. "It just seems wrong somehow. Everybody has rights, and just because somebody is stronger than you, they shouldn't be allowed to run your life and push you around. That's what we think, anyway. Don't you?"

John didn't answer me. A strange, thoughtful look came over his face. I was puzzled. One moment we were all laughing and talking together, and the next he seemed to have detached himself as though we weren't there. Without a word, he got up and began to pile our glasses and plates back on the tray. My bubble of happiness was rudely punctured. I was afraid he had had enough of us. Maybe all rich people were like this, indulging themselves with whims that took them on the spur of the moment, and tiring of them just as quickly.

Uncertainly, I said, "I think we'd better go now. It's getting late."

He didn't try to stop us. He showed us to the door, and I could have cried. It wasn't ending at all the way it should have, and I had no idea at all what had gone wrong. Hesitating in the doorway, I tried to thank him.

"That's all right," he said, looking over my head. "It's nice to find someone spunky enough to stand up for what they believe in. I envy you."

I stared at him, bewildered, thinking he must be making fun of me again, but there was no laughter in his eyes this time. They looked withdrawn and unhappy. The boys were already running down the driveway.

"Goodnight, Joanna," he said, turning away from me. "I'll see you on Saturday, then."

I was left standing on the doorstep, with the closed door between us. My head was whirling around in confusion. Slowly I followed after Julian and Maxwell, who were waiting for me by the road, bubbling with excitement. Nobody would have thought they had just lost their allowance and had to work for nothing in the bargain. They were not as sensitive as I was, and hadn't noticed that they had been given the cold shoulder.

"I knew everything would turn out okay," burbled Maxwell ecstatically. "I just knew it!"

"You're crazy," I told him.

"So are you," he said. "You're just as crazy as we are."

I sighed deeply and gave him a sad smile. "Yes," I said. "I believe I am."

The Horse Show

· 7 ·

Grandma thought that we had just gone out and got ourselves jobs, and she was very proud of us.

"I hope you put your money in the bank," she said, "and don't fritter it away on trifles."

We could assure her truthfully that we wouldn't be frittering anything away. Our wages would all be spent before we earned them, but of course we couldn't tell her that. Anyway, I would gladly have worked at Holmwood Farms for nothing, just to be surrounded by those beautiful horses.

On Saturday morning I made myself look as nice and practical as possible and set off as soon as I had done the breakfast dishes. John was doing practice jumps in the ring as I came down into the paddock. He saw me and waved. He was riding a big black gelding I hadn't seen before.

"Morning!" he called out. "My grandfather's expecting

you. You'll find him in the big barn. One of the mares foaled last night."

"Where's Queenie?" I called back.

"We have a show at Erinvale this afternoon. She's gone ahead in the trailer."

"Well, good luck," I said enviously. If it had been me entering a horse show that afternoon, I would have been a mass of nerves and excitement, but John didn't seem too concerned. I suppose when you did something often enough, it became commonplace, but I didn't think I would ever feel that way.

He went back to his jumping and, remembering what a stickler for punctuality John's father had been, I thought I had better get a move on.

I found old Mr. Holmes in one of the stalls with Jim and John's father. The new foal was teetering around on knobby legs, bumping into everything. Jim was trying to persuade it to drink from its mother, a beautiful gray Hunter with placid eyes who seemed bored by the whole business. They didn't see me for a moment, and I hung over the stall, fascinated by the new baby, and wishing it could have been mine—a horse of my very own to love and cherish. Then John's father turned and saw me.

"Good morning," he said crisply. I didn't know whether he remembered me or not. I was a bit afraid of him. I was glad when old Mr. Holmes took me into a small office adjacent to the barn. He, at least, was friendly.

"So you want to work here, do you?" he said. "I'm sure we can find something for you to do. Have you worked much with horses?"

"Not really," I told him, "but I love them. And I don't mind what I do."

He smiled at me, showing approval. "That's the spirit!

John tells me you want to make a couple of dollars' extra pocket money. Is that right?"

I nodded again and he said, "Well we usually pay a dollar an hour to students for mucking out the barn and doing things like that. Would that suit you? Say, from eight to twelve every Saturday morning."

That would be four dollars a week! Not only would I earn the two dollars needed for Horse, but I would have an extra two dollars to share between the boys and me, so that we could still buy a few treats to make life less austere.

"Oh that would be marvelous!" I said.

He looked at me curiously. I suppose he wasn't used to people going into transports of joy over such a small amount of money, but he couldn't begin to imagine what it meant to me.

"Very well," he said. "You can start this morning if you like. You'll be working for Jim. We have to leave for the horse show shortly, but he'll fix you up before he goes."

He went out and returned with Jim, who took me in charge.

"How's the leg, sweetheart?" he asked me as we walked through the big barn together.

"Fine," I told him.

"That's good. We'll get you to clean out the empty stalls and replace the shavings this morning. I hope you don't mind hard work."

"Not a bit," I said eagerly.

"John took your horse over to the other place yesterday, in case you're wondering."

I had been dying to ask, but didn't know whether I should. I wasn't sure how much Jim had been told. "Thanks for looking after her," I said, "I don't know if John told you. . . ."

He cut me off short. "Sweetheart, I never ask questions. I do exactly as I'm told, okay?"

His eyes twinkled at me, and I felt reassured. "But if anybody should ask you. . . ."

"Then they'll find I have a very short memory," he said, smiling to himself.

Our secret formed a sort of a bond between us, and we got along famously right from the start. I did work hard and by noon my back was aching, but I enjoyed every minute of it. With four dollars in my pocket, I ran home happily to tell my family about it. Wallace Pindlebury's car was parked in our driveway. I found him draped over the rocker in the kitchen watching Margaret and the boys eat lunch. He was a bit like Horse in that he never stood when he could lean, and never sat when he could sprawl.

Grandma was baking and the kitchen smelled of hot buns. When I had cleaned up, I helped myself to a big bowl of soup and regaled them all with an account of my morning. Grandma, Julian and Maxwell were most interested, but Margaret felt overshadowed. She said to Wallace, "Everyone in this family is getting terribly horsey suddenly. If you don't talk horse talk, nobody listens to you anymore. Maybe we should go to the horse show this afternoon. Then they might talk to us again."

"When I was ten years old," remarked Wallace, casually picking his teeth, "I produced a literary masterpiece, my only one. It went something like this:

A horse it is a noble beast,
I love to stand beside one,
But God and all the saints forbid
That I should ever ride one.

70

And those," he finished, "are my sentiments where horses are concerned. But if that's where the action is, man, that's where we'll go."

Margaret jumped up and gave him a kiss. I wondered if I gave him one, too, whether he would take me with them, but I doubted it. I was green with envy. "Wallace," I pleaded, "if you take me with you I'll do anything you want me to, honest I will."

"I don't want anything doing," he said, quite unmoved.

"Oh, please!" I begged him. "I'll sit in the back seat and be as quiet as a mouse. I'll even lie down on the floor so you can't see me, if you like. I'll even curl up in the trunk!"

"I don't think," he said dispassionately, looking me up and down, "that you'd fit in."

"Oh, you're mean!" I cried out. "What do you want me to do, grovel in front of you and kiss your boots?"

"Oh, take her, or she'll never shut up," said Margaret impatiently. "But you get lost, Jo, when we're there. I'm fed up with my family tagging along wherever I go."

I promised joyously that I would disappear and they would not set eyes on me until they were ready to return. I was radiant with excitement at the thought of seeing John perform. I paid my entrance fee out of my two-dollar bonus, putting the rest away for Julian and Maxwell. Then I lost myself in the crowd. The atmosphere at the showground was wonderful to me. I breathed it into my pores. Everywhere were horses and horse people. Unabashed, I listened in on conversations, hearing things like conformation, style and gait discussed, words that I didn't completely understand but was determined I would soon. I would get books from the library and read up on everything there was to know about horses. I saw girls my own age, slim as reeds in their peaked velvet

71

hard hats, waisted jackets and jodhpurs, riding beautiful horses. They were so sure of themselves, blessed with good looks and poise. They inhabited a different world from mine, a world that I could only guess at, into which only the fortunate and wealthy were permitted to enter. Certainly the Joanna Longfellows of this world were not among them.

When the senior jumping competitions were announced, I pushed myself to the very front of the crowd, determined that I wasn't going to miss seeing John. I had butterflies in my stomach when his name was called out. "Queen of the Nile, owned by Holmwood Farms, ridden by John Holmes!" I saw them come into the ring, and I had never seen Queenie look so elegant with her mane and tail plaited, and her coat shining like silk. I could feel the power in her as she surged over the jumps. Once she nicked a pole but it didn't fall. I thought they made the other jumpers look like amateurs, but it was a beautiful blonde girl who walked away with the red ribbon. John came in second. How I hated that girl! I watched John leading Queenie out, the blue rosette attached to her bridle. His shoulders drooped slightly. I squeezed out of the stands and made my way to the competitors' enclosure, hoping I would be able to speak to him for a minute.

There were so many horses and people, horse trailers and wagons about that I didn't know where to go. Then I caught sight of Jim leading Queenie but, before I could reach him, I saw John talking with his father and grandfather. My courage failed me. I didn't feel up to meeting the whole family, so I lurked behind a trailer, hoping I would get a chance to see John alone later.

I hadn't meant to eavesdrop, but I couldn't help it. John's father was pulling him to pieces. Everything about the way he had jumped was criticized. There was not one word of praise or encouragement. Even his grandfather added some opinions, but less harshly. Listening, I got angrier by the minute. John, I noticed, was not even trying to stand up for himself.

"Look at the fiasco at the Royal last year!" I heard his father say. "You disgraced our name there, John! People don't expect that kind of riding from a Holmes. Your whole trouble is lack of discipline. You're too easily satisfied with second-best. There was absolutely no reason why you couldn't have come first in that jump if your heart had been in it! If you go on like this, you won't even be eligible for the Royal this year. I can't tell you, John, what a disappointment you are to me!"

"I'm sorry, Father." John's voice was low and sullen. "Believe it or not, I was doing my best. I know what it means to you. You've told me often enough."

"Then obviously your best isn't good enough," answered Mr. Holmes curtly. "I'm sorry to keep on at you, John, but it's for your own good. Now go and relax for a while. You're on again at four o'clock, so let's see if we can do better then, shall we?"

They turned away, as an acquaintance hailed them, leaving John alone. He started to walk away, the droop in his shoulders more pronounced than ever. I ran into step beside him and blurted out, "John, I saw you and Queenie jump, and I thought you were terrific, I really did! You would have been first if it hadn't been for that silly pole. I thought you were marvelous."

He turned and stared at me as though I had dropped from the sky. "I didn't know you were going to be here, Joanna," he said.

73

"I didn't know either," I told him. "But I'm glad I saw you jump. It was so exciting. You looked so good together, you and Queenie."

His black expression lightened, and he even managed a smile. "Thanks, Joanna. You should have been one of the judges. Unfortunately, your opinion wasn't shared by everybody, but I must say it's nice to have a fan club of one. How did you get here?"

"My sister's boyfriend brought me," I told him and added darkly, "under pressure, of course."

John chuckled. "I'd like to meet the rest of your family. I got a kick out of your brothers."

"You did?" I was truly astonished. "I thought—I thought. . . ."

"You thought what?"

Clumsily, I heard myself saying, "I thought you'd had enough of us the other night."

He shook his head, smiling, but the hurt was still in his eyes. He must still be remembering what his father had said to him. If it had been me, I would have cried for days.

"Why don't you come to our house, then?" I said impulsively. "You don't have to have an invitation. Anybody pops in whenever they want."

"Maybe I'll just do that," he said. We stood looking at each other for a moment. Then he touched my shoulder briefly and said, "I'd better go, Joanna. I'm on again soon. Thank you for cheering me up."

I smiled at him shyly. "And thank you for taking Horse. Jim told me."

"That's all right," he said, "and by the way, Joanna, if you want to use our swimming pool during the week, please do. It's just sitting there, doing nothing."

Before I could thank him, he lifted his hand at me and

74

was lost in the crowd. I stood still, my head spinning. I just had to break my promise and go looking for Margaret and Wallace to tell them the news. It was lucky I did because they were looking for me.

"We've got to go now," Margaret said. "We're going to a party tonight, and we don't want to be late."

I was disappointed I wouldn't see John ride again, but I climbed into the car obediently. When I told Margaret about the swimming pool she raised her eyebrows and said, "Wow, we are moving in high circles, aren't we? Be careful we don't fall down with a bad bump and hurt ourselves."

"You can use it, too, if you want to," I said.

"Oh? Well kindly convey to the Holmeses that I would be delighted to grace their pool with my humble presence," she said airily, but I think she was secretly pleased.

"Did you enjoy the horse show?" I asked her.

"Yes," she said. "It was very horsey."

I couldn't get anything else out of her, but that didn't upset me. I kept thinking about John Holmes wanting to come over to our house, and about using his pool, and I felt so tingly and nice inside, I was ready to love everybody, even Wallace Pindlebury.

We Are Found Out

· 8 ·

After a few weeks things seemed to have settled down, and we became complacent. Julian had his bicycle repaired with the ten dollars I hadn't used on the taxi, and twice a week he and Maxwell cycled over to Horse's new home to work for her keep. When I didn't have homework I went with them, to take Horse a treat and talk to her, so she wouldn't forget me. She had made friends with another mare boarded there, and they leaned on each other nose to tail, keeping the flies away. Coming home, we would park our bicycles at Holmwood Farms and go for a swim. It was like having our own pool. The housekeeper learned to expect us, and she would bring out snacks, which we devoured like savages. Looking after horses was hungry work.

On other evenings I would sometimes pop over to the stables to see Jim. We were great friends now. He was giving me all sorts of tips on riding, and sometimes he would let me exercise some of the more docile horses in the ring. There had been no more word from Mr. Crossley, which surprised us, but we did see an announcement in the local paper that Mr. Archer had left the hospital and was convalescing at the home of his nephew in Kitchener. We just took it for granted, I suppose, that we had averted trouble and that, before long, Mr. Archer would return and take Horse off our hands. The three of us were having such a good time, it seemed only natural to be optimistic.

John had come to visit us, as he said he would, the Friday evening after the horse show. Grandma had spent all day making strawberry preserves, and during the last batch the kettle had developed a leak, pouring gooey syrup all over the burner and down the side of the stove. When John's knock on the door came, the kitchen was full of vicious black smoke, a pool of preserves was spreading over the floor and, with our usual lack of coordination, we were all running around in panic.

I was absolutely aghast to see John. I almost pushed him out again, but he had taken in everything at a glance and, with wonderful presence of mind, he flung open the window, rushed into the yard with the leaking pot, and organized a cleanup operation. I was mortified to have him catch us in such a state, but he actually seemed to be enjoying himself. Grandma was charmed by him. "Good breeding always comes to the fore in emergencies," she told me, which made me feel that I had been brought up in the gutter. But it was funny afterward and, although I didn't see much of John now that the horse show circuit had started, he often stuck his head around the stall I was cleaning and asked innocently, "Anyone making jam at your house today?" It became a private joke shared between the two of us.

So June passed cheerfully in a succession of warm,

happy days. When I walked over to Holmwood Farms it was knee-deep in alfalfa, which perfumed the air with a vague sweet scent and attracted hundreds of bees. We were lulled into a state of contentment, but we should have known that in our family nothing ever went smoothly for long.

On the first day of our summer holiday Grandma had a letter from Mother, which she read to us over lunch. She had hoped to be home for her birthday in July, but now they expected to be away for another two or three months. Their research had gone slower than they had expected because Father was enjoying going native. The letter sounded a bit wistful, and Grandma shook her head over it.

"Your poor mother," she said. "You can tell she misses you. She never was one for roughing it. If it wasn't for your father, I don't think she'd ever leave home again."

This was startling news to me. "Well, why doesn't she stay home, so we wouldn't have to be moving every five minutes?" I asked, genuinely surprised. "Dad could go on his trips by himself."

Grandma looked knowing. "Wait until you're married, dear. And I hope you have sense enough to fall for someone who isn't always gadding halfway across the world. Don't you think you should send your mother a nice birthday present, something special, to cheer her up?"

"I saw a most gorgeous negligee in a boutique in Kitchener," Margaret said helpfully. "Hot pink, with purple flounces on the sleeves. Absolutely dreamy!"

We stared at her.

"Hot pink!" gulped Grandma at last. "With *purple* flounces?"

"Why not? What's wrong with that?"

Grandma blinked. "Well, dear, for a tent, don't you think . . . ?"

78

"Exactly!" cut in Margaret with authority. "She must be fed up with dirty old slacks and shirts. I know that's what *I'd* like. Something to make me feel like a woman," she added, as though that settled the matter once and for all.

"Well," demurred Grandma, "I suppose you do have a point there. But I think you should get it soon and send it off in plenty of time, so she'll have it for her birthday. Is that all right with the rest of you?"

We must have been bemused, for, even then, the question of money never occurred to us. We nodded and said it was fine as long as Margaret made it clear to Mother that it was her choice, not ours.

"Okay," said Margaret. "Wallace is taking me into Kitchener on Saturday, so I'll get it then. It's marked down to twenty dollars, so I'll want five dollars from each of you."

"Five dollars!" Maxwell, Julian and I all echoed her together, in a sort of stupefied horror as the situation dawned on us. Grandma and Margaret must have been thinking we were stashing away money from our part-time jobs, since we weren't buying anything, when in actual fact we didn't have any money at all—not even our weekly allowances! Everything had gone on Horse, except the extra two dollars I made, which was split three ways and was eaten up almost at once.

"Couldn't we just make her something?" I said in a sickly voice. "She likes the things we make ourselves, she's always said so."

Margaret looked at each of us, and an expression of disgust crossed her face. "Don't tell me you begrudge five dollars each for your own mother!" she exploded. "Of all the penny-pinching little misers. . . . How mean can you get?"

We stared at her, sick with dismay. Our silence only made a worse impression. Even Grandma looked surprised.

"I don't think five dollars each is too much to spend on

your mother," she said sternly. "When I said don't fritter your money away, I didn't mean you had to hoard it. Surely you'd be willing to part with a little to make your own mother happy, wouldn't you?"

Still we didn't answer, because we couldn't. Inside I was squirming. I saw Grandma's lips go tight with disapproval. "Very well," she said at last, "I shall give Margaret the fifteen dollars. I must say I wouldn't have believed it of you three, but I'd rather your mother didn't know you were too mean to part with a penny of your earnings to give her a bit of happiness."

That made me feel worse, because I knew Grandma wasn't rolling in money. Still I couldn't think of any excuse to make that would sound legitimate. The boys must have felt just as bad, because the next thing I knew Maxwell was bawling. I hadn't seen Maxwell cry since he was a baby.

"We've got to tell them!" he wailed. "We've got to!"

"Shut up!" hissed Julian, kicking him under the table, which only made Maxwell cry harder.

"We don't have any money!" he blubbered. "We're not mean. We're keeping Horse for Mr. Archer. All our money's gone on Horse!"

Julian and I groaned in unison, but I think that if Maxwell hadn't confessed I would have. I couldn't bear to see Grandma and Margaret looking at us in that way.

There was a stunned silence in the kitchen. Then Grandma looked at me and said quietly, "Joanna, perhaps you'd better explain."

I had no choice. I stumbled through the whole sorry story, watching Grandma's outrage grow by the minute.

"How could you!" she exclaimed. "Really, Joanna, the whole thing's deceitful from beginning to end! I can't believe you would be party to such a trick, and that poor Mr. Crossley almost beside himself with worry over Horse! Really—I don't know what to say!"

I was peeved. Once again I was bearing the brunt for what had been the boys' idea. "I don't think it was so terrible," I said sullenly. "We got that note from Mr. Archer and made it legal. We couldn't have been arrested or anything."

Grandma let out her breath sharply. "It's the deceitful way you went about it, telling lies to that poor man and giving him all that trouble and worry when he was only doing what he thought best. And scheming behind my back, too, like three—like three juvenile delinquents! I can't believe it of you!"

"But everything's worked out all right," I ventured timidly.

"Everything is not all right!" replied Grandma with emphasis. "Mr. Archer isn't a young man, and he may never be able to look after himself again. And even if he comes back to his house, it won't be for some time, I can assure you. When you're over seventy, broken bones take a long time to mend. So what happens when your parents return? Who's going to pay for Horse's board after you've gone? Really, I can't begin to think! My head is spinning!"

We sat in disgrace, our heads hanging, waiting for Grandma's verdict. At last she stood up and said with purpose, "Well, what's happened has happened, and there's only one thing to be done now—bring it out in the open and see where we go from there! You can't pile deceit upon deceit and hope to get away with it. Eventually it'll catch up with you. Apart from all that, it's quite ridiculous, this business of spending all your allowance on keeping someone else's horse boarded, not to mention working for nothing!"

She went into the hall and came back with her hat jammed squarely on her head.

"Where are you going, Grandma?" I asked nervously.

"I'm going to see Mr. Crossley," she informed me. "I've got his address from the paper, and it'll be up to him and Mr. Archer to decide what's to happen about Horse, as it should have been in the first place. I'm sorry, children, but I hope this will be a lesson to you in future not to meddle in things that don't concern you."

Very upset, her white curls bobbing, she stalked out of the house. A minute later we heard her old car backfire and go puttering down the driveway. Margaret took pity on our miserable faces.

"Cheer up," she said. "You couldn't have gotten away with it indefinitely. You'd soon get fed up with not having any money, anyway, you know you would."

She didn't understand that sometimes it was possible to love someone or something so much that sacrifices weren't sacrifices at all, and that's how we felt about Horse. We had hardly missed our allowances.

"Well at least," said Maxwell in a voice of doom, "they can't put us in prison. We didn't steal Horse. We had Mr. Archer's note."

But somehow that didn't seem so consoling anymore. All we could do was wait out the rest of the day, stiff with worry and unhappiness, waiting for Grandma to return and pronounce sentence on us and Horse.

Our Household Increases

· 9 ·

When Grandma had not returned by evening we felt that boded no good for us. We decided to go to bed early in the hope that overnight everybody might cool down a bit. I hadn't expected to sleep, but the next thing I knew it was broad daylight, and I could smell coffee brewing. Maxwell and Julian were still asleep. I thought I had better find out what had happened as soon as possible. Putting on my housecoat, I went downstairs to find Grandma and Mr. Archer having a cozy little tête-à-tête over coffee and toast in the kitchen. I was so surprised, I stood in the doorway and goggled.

Grandma saw me first, and I'll swear she looked a bit sheepish. "Oh, Joanna," she said, "you remember Mr. Archer, don't you?"

"Well I remember this young lady," said Mr. Archer,

beaming at me, "even if I were a bit doped up at the time. How are you, my dear?"

Still in a daze, I mumbled that I was fine. Mr. Archer looked good, too, much better than when I had last seen him, but I noticed crutches beside his chair.

"Well, don't stand there gawking," Grandma chided me briskly. "Where are your manners? Come and have some breakfast." She set me a place and said, "I suppose you're wondering what's going on?"

That had to be the understatement of the year. "What's happened to Mr. Crossley?" I ventured timidly, half-expecting him to crawl out from under the table. "And what about Horse?"

Grandma sat down and let out a long deep sigh. "Well, Joanna," she said reluctantly, "much as I hate to say this, you were right about Mr. Crossley. He is not a gentleman at all. He said some very unpleasant things to me, particularly regarding you children and, while they might have been justified, I didn't think it was his place to say them. I'm afraid I got a little annoyed."

Mr. Archer chuckled and winked at me. "That she did! She's a spunky woman is your grandma. My nephew hadn't let on a thing about Horse, let me think she was still at the house. 'Uncle,' he says to me, 'I've this young couple need to rent a house for a year, so how about letting them have yours, then they can keep an eye on the horse when those kids have to leave their grandma's?' So of course I agrees, thinking it's a good idea, and then your grandma turns up yesterday and tells me that Horse hasn't been there for over a month. Why, I couldn't believe it! I'd never have rented the house if I'd known. I only did it on account of Horse, but if I'd known she were lost, by golly, I'd have crawled back on my hands and knees if I'd had to, and gone searching for her. Seems like he'd figured on that, and was afraid of losing a buck. I've had my eyes opened, I can tell you!"

"That's what Margaret said!" I exclaimed triumphantly. "You see, Grandma, we were right! Except we thought he wanted to sell your house."

Mr. Archer's face looked grim for a moment. "Aye, and he might have done that, too, after the year's lease were up. He was right put out when your grandma told him Horse weren't lost at all. I reckon he were hoping she'd gone for good. More or less called me an old fool for wanting to hang on to Horse and the farm, and told me to act my age. 'Sonny boy,' I says to him, 'when you're my age I hope you're half as spry as I am—you'll be doing all right!' Then your grandma, bless her, says, 'You don't have to take that kind of talk. Why, I've a spare room at my house, you come and board with me until that young couple's lease is up!' So up I gets and walks out! Told him he's welcome to keep the rent for the house, since he's fixed it up a bit, and I don't want him to be out of pocket on account of me, but I says to him, 'After that, don't you come around bothering me no more, because I don't take kindly to being made a fool of, especially by my own kin.' So here I am!"

I noticed that both he and Grandma were looking mightily pleased with themselves. Our misdeeds seemed to have been forgotten in their glow of righteousness, and I was very pleased to leave it that way.

"I think that's just wonderful!" I said, and meant it. "Welcome to our house, Mr. Archer!"

"Well, thank you my dear," he said with old-fashioned courtliness. "And Horse and me, why, we'll always be grateful for what you and your young rapscallion brothers have done for us. I've only my pension, and by the time I've paid your grandma for my board and bought a few oats for

Horse and a bit of tobacco for myself, there'll not be much change left from a dollar but, whatever there is, you children shall have first claim to it, you rest assured about that!"

"Oh, Mr. Archer, we don't want to be paid back!" I exclaimed indignantly. "We did it because we loved Horse! What's going to happen to her now, anyway?"

"We've been talking about that," said Grandma. "I've a perfectly good field going begging at the back here, and there's no reason why she can't stay out there for the present."

"Oh, Grandma!" I cried, jumping up and giving her a hug. "You're the greatest! You really are!"

She looked embarrassed but pleased. "Oh, don't be silly, Joanna," she protested. "The field's there. It might as well be used. Of course, I don't know what we'll do when winter comes. The old barn is no shelter at all. Still, we'll cross our bridges when we come to them."

I sat down again, feeling suddenly subdued. It had just come home to me that we wouldn't be here when winter came. The thought was anguish to me. No more riding, no more John, no more Horse. For a moment I didn't think I could bear it. I almost wished that something would happen to keep my parents in Mexico indefinitely. Then I was afraid my wish might be granted literally and some accident would befall them so that I would never see them again, and that was a pretty horrible thought, too. I was near tears at that moment, thinking of life going on at Holmwood Farms without me and, if Maxwell and Julian hadn't come creeping into the kitchen, looking so guilty it was laughable, I might have disgraced myself by bawling. The boys' reaction at the sight of Mr. Archer was even more startled than mine. The story had to be repeated, and then again for the benefit of

Margaret, who always chose to float languidly downstairs after everyone had finished breakfast.

While we were all talking at once, as usual, the doorbell rang. We all stopped in midsentence and looked at one another in consternation. I think everyone's first thought was that it was Mr. Crossley come to make trouble. Grandma got up to open the door, and there stood Wallace Pindlebury. He came in, giving us the peace sign. "Greetings," he said. "I hope I'm not disturbing this jolly little family party."

Margaret, who had dived under the table to pull the rollers hastily out of her hair, rose looking rather frizzy and wild, and said petulantly, "Goodness, Wallace, it's only half-past eight! What are you doing here so early?"

"I was kind of wondering," he said, "if you would let me sleep in your barn, as a temporary arrangement, of course, just for the summer?"

This took a moment to sink in, then Grandma, gathering her wits about her, asked him if he was serious. He was so rarely serious, it was not as silly a question as it sounded. But this time he was. It seemed that his father had finally agreed to pay his tuition at the summer art school, which was located not far from where we lived but, when Wallace had gone up there last night to register, he found that the fees, which were expensive enough, did not include board and lodging.

"And there's no way, man," he exclaimed in despair, "that I'm going to get another penny out of my old man! He was dead-set against summer school from the start. Wanted me to go and get a job." He looked even paler than usual at the ghastly thought. "I had to practically break his arm to get him to agree. Now I find the fees don't include any extras and, if I ask him for another forty dollars a week, he's going

87

to blow his mind. So, I thought of your old barn. It would be a roof over my head and that's all I need, and maybe a few leftovers in the way of food for sustenance. I am not," he said with pathos, "a hard person to please."

"Well, I'm sure you're not, dear," agreed Grandma, rather startled. "But you can't sleep in that old barn. It doesn't have any walls, and the roof must leak in a hundred places. Oh, dear, it never rains but it pours! You'd have been quite welcome to stay with us, but now here's Mr. Archer taken over the spare room, and I have no idea where to put you. Unless . . . ." She turned to me, and I felt something ominous in the wind. "Unless, Joanna dear, you wouldn't mind Margaret moving in with you. You've got a nice double bed in your room. Then Wallace could have Margaret's. I hate to think of him with nowhere to go."

My heart sank. I knew what sharing a room with Margaret was like—manuscripts all over the place, the dresser covered with nail polish, curlers and makeup, and Margaret pacing the floor at midnight in the throes of being inspired. Then I realized that everybody in the room was looking at me expectantly. They were all feeling so good about Mr. Archer and Horse, they wanted everybody, including Wallace, to share in our happiness. I couldn't be petty enough to refuse.

"Okay," I said to Margaret, trying to sound gracious. "But if you hog all the bedclothes, I'll kick you out of bed!"

Margaret instantly jumped up and hugged me. I could never remember her doing that before, and I was touched. Being unselfish wasn't so painful after all.

With our family growing at the rate of one an hour, we were not really surprised when the doorbell rang again. I wondered if this time it would turn out to be Mr. Crossley, and whether he was going to ask to move in with us as well.

This time we all felt so united, we didn't care if it was Mr. Crossley or not. I went to the door and had the nicest surprise of the morning. John stood there giving me his nice, lopsided smile.

I hadn't expected to see him down early this week, because I knew he was learning the ropes in his father's business now that university was out. Then I remembered there was an important Class A show coming up in a couple of weeks, and he probably had to get in all the practice he could. This particular show could be the deciding factor in whether or not he would be eligible for the Royal Horse Show this year. John's father was really riding him about this one.

"May I come in?" he asked. "I won't have much time to myself for the rest of the weekend, so I thought I'd pop in now and say hello, and maybe scrounge a cup of coffee."

We had to introduce him to Mr. Archer, and by that time our simple breakfast had taken on the air of a festive occasion. None of us wanted to break it up, so John suggested we continue our celebration over at his pool. We all thought this was a great idea. We collected our bathing suits and left Grandma and Mr. Archer in peace.

Dew was still sparkling on the grass as we walked over the fields. Bobolinks perched on the swaying stems, scolding us, and in the blue vault of the sky a red-tailed hawk hung motionless. I felt madly happy for no particular reason, all my gloomy thoughts banished.

"Oh," I said impulsively, "I wish this morning could go on for ever and ever and ever!"

John looked at me affectionately. "No you don't, Joanna," he said, "because you'd soon get bored with it if it did. That's human nature."

Maybe he was right, but I didn't want to believe him.

We were all so in tune with each other for once. Margaret had festooned Wallace with dandelion chains, and the gesture must have made him want to reciprocate. Picking a three-foot stalk of chicory, with one tiny blue flower on top, he presented it to me ceremoniously and said, "Peace."

"Peace to you, too," I said, and stuck it in my belt where it trailed down and tickled my ankles. The horrible fact was that I was beginning to be quite fond of Wallace, in a sisterly sort of way. I suppose you can get used to anything if you're subjected to it long enough.

In the exercise ring, Jim was trying out the new Thoroughbred which had arrived that morning from Florida. He pulled up to let us admire her. She was sleek and beautiful, more slender and less powerful than Queenie, but a real champion. We could almost see our faces in the gloss of her chestnut flanks. John told us his father was branching out into Thoroughbreds as well as Hunters, and she was to be used as a brood mare.

"Are you going to let me exercise her, Jim?" I teased him.

I hadn't expected for a moment to be taken seriously, but he was quite serious when he said, "I might just do that. I've been watching your progress lately, Joanna, and you're really coming along."

This was a compliment indeed, and quite unexpected. The others looked at me with new respect. John, especially, seemed surprised. He stared at me with an odd look on his face.

"Is she *that* good, Jim?"

"You bet she is. You'll have to watch it, John, or she'll be stealing some of those ribbons away from you soon."

"Oh, he's kidding!" I protested. I was so embarrassed I didn't know where to look.

"I don't think so. I think he means it." There was something strange in the way John was looking at me and in the sudden lowering of his voice. All at once, without any explanation, he said, "I'd better get Queenie tacked up. You know where to go. Have a good time," and he was gone.

Watching him striding away to the big barn, abandoning us without a backward look, my heart sank into my shoes. Why did Jim have to say that just then? Any other time it would have made me so proud, but I didn't want John to think I was some little upstart, trying to upstage him.

"What's eating him?" asked Wallace, voicing all our thoughts.

"I don't know. Sometimes I don't understand him at all," I confessed miserably. "He gets moody for no reason."

"He's jealous of you," said Margaret smugly. "He's a Holmes, remember? They don't like to think that anybody could be better than they are."

"Oh, but I'm not! I never could be!" I protested vehemently. "Jim was only teasing. Surely John could see that!"

Margaret shrugged. "I expect he's insecure. That's why he's got to be the best all the time. Lots of rich people are basically insecure because they think it's only their money that's making them somebody."

"Oh, baloney!" I retorted. "How do you know? You've never been rich!"

Margaret stuck her nose in the air. "I'm a writer," she reminded me rather pointlessly, since she never let us forget it. "I have to make it my business to study characteristics of people."

But, whatever she said, I couldn't believe that about John, and the fact that he might be jealous of me would have been almost laughable if I hadn't seen the way he had acted with my own eyes. His abrupt departure dampened our spirits somewhat but, once we were in the water, we perked up. Having that lovely pool all to ourselves made us feel like millionaires. The housekeeper fed us, as usual, and later on John, having gotten over whatever ailed him, took some time off to have a swim with us. He was his usual friendly self again, and so hospitable toward us that I began to think that I had exaggerated the whole incident.

A Confusing Talk with John

· 10 ·

Jim brought Horse back that week. We lined up on the driveway and cheered as her ample rear backed slowly out of the narrow trailer. The nice thing about Horse was that she took everything in her stride. Nothing made her nervous. She ambled right over to Mr. Archer and began inspecting his crutches, no doubt thinking they were some new strain of gigantic carrot.

Once she was installed in the back field, things settled down to a fairly normal routine again, and it was surprising how well we all got along with each other. I think it was because we were all happy. Maxwell, Julian and Mr. Archer were happy because they had Horse back, and Grandma was happy to have someone of her own generation to talk to for a change. Margaret was happy to have Wallace right under her thumb, and Wallace was happy because he was spared the awful shock of having to earn forty dollars a week. He was so grateful to Grandma he took over the care of her potted plants to test his theory that, if you sang to plants, they would respond. Oddly enough they did, too. They began to run riot, blocking out daylight from the windows. We finally had to move them into the sun porch where they formed a small jungle which threatened to engulf Wallace, who was usually found sitting in the middle of them, meditating.

As for me, I was probably the happiest of the lot. I had kept my job at Holmwood Farms because I loved it. Jim was giving me more responsibility, and I had more opportunity to ride. I even exercised the Thoroughbred, as Jim had promised, and that was a great day for me.

One evening, Maxwell, Julian and I were sitting on the fence, feeding Horse dandelion leaves and clover, when Maxwell said, "You know what? I think Horse is lucky. Good things happen when she's around. Nobody shouts at anybody anymore. Everybody's nice!"

I laughed, but in a way it was true. "Maybe she's a magic horse. Perhaps when Mother and Dad come back she'll bewitch them into wanting to settle down right here. Wouldn't that be terrific?"

"Oh, don't kid yourself!" retorted Julian, impatient with fantasies. "Can you see Dad settling down in the country? You've forgotten what he's like. Places bore him after six months, even cities. I reckon he'd last one week here, and that's all, if there was anywhere for them to stay, which there isn't."

I knew it was true, but I was annoyed with Julian for always being so rational. It was a nice thought to believe that roly-poly, silly old Horse could look at people with her velvet-brown eyes and bring contentment into their lives.

"I think we ought to build her a barn," said Maxwell out of the blue.

Julian and I nearly fell off the fence. "You're nuts!" said Julian.

"Well, fix up the old one, then. I know we won't be here in the winter, but you know Grandma and Mr. Archer don't have any money, and I wouldn't want to think of Horse being out in the cold all winter. I'd never sleep, thinking about her." He hugged Horse's neck and blew gently up her nostrils as though he were already trying to warm her.

Julian and I were subdued by his unselfishness. Because we knew we weren't going to be around to enjoy Horse, we had ceased to concern ourselves with her future. Now Maxwell made us feel ashamed. Scowling and chewing vigorously on his thumbnail, a procedure which aided his thought processes, Julian said, "Maybe we could get enough good wood from the old barn to build a new small barn, just big enough for Horse. Mr. Archer knows about building barns. He told us when he was a kid they used to have barn-raising bees. All the farmers for miles around pitched in to help, and they made a party of it. He could tell us what to do, and we could do the work."

I hated to be a wet blanket, but now it was my turn to be realistic. "Julian, even if we salvaged wood from the old barn, to put on the outside, we'd need new wood for the frame, and then there'd be the foundation and the doors and the windows. I bet we'd have to spend a hundred dollars at least. Even if we saved our allowances again, it would still take months to save up enough, and you know that we don't have that much time left."

Although I was forcing myself to accept the fact, it still hurt to say it. Julian and Maxwell didn't want to hear it either. Julian went on scowling at his shoes, and Maxwell played absentmindedly with Horse's ears.

"Hey!" said Julian suddenly, "I've got an idea. People

95

sell things for good causes. Well, Horse is a good cause. Let's put up a stall at Kitchener Market and take Horse with us. We could put up a sign telling all about her and what we're selling things for. If she looked at people with those big eyes of hers, I bet they couldn't resist buying something to help her, even if they didn't particularly want it."

"Want what?" asked Maxwell stupidly.

"Whatever we're selling, you moron!"

"But what would we be selling?"

"Oh, anything!" exclaimed Julian, impatient with such trivial details. "There's tons of stuff in the garden—flowers and currants and junk like that, and some of Gran's jam, and those painted bottles you made at school. You can sell anything at a market; it doesn't matter."

"Now wait a minute!" I protested. "Won't you ever learn, Julian? You and your crazy ideas! Haven't you got us into enough trouble this summer already? The whole idea's absolutely idiotic!"

Julian gave me his icy stare, reserved usually for obtuse adults. "Why is it idiotic?"

"Because it is, you idiot! You don't just walk into the market with a bunch of stuff and sell it, that's why! You'd probably have to hire a stall for the whole season, and go on a waiting list to get one, and then I think you have to have a license to sell, because of sales tax or something like that. I don't know all the rules. I just know it's not as simple as just walking in, setting up a stall and that's that!"

I should explain about Kitchener Market, which is quite famous in our part of the country. Once a week the local farmers, mostly Mennonites, bring in their produce to sell and, because it's good and fresh and their womenfolk bake wonderful bread, cakes and pies, people come from as far away as Toronto to be there by six o'clock on Saturday morning when it opens. By eight o'clock nearly all the perishable stuff has gone, but there are still home-cured meats, hams and sausage, free-range chickens and freshly plucked geese, goose eggs and sauerkraut, and countless other goodies too numerous to mention. Then there are handicrafts, painstakingly and beautifully worked by the Mennonite women. In fact, the Kitchener Market is an institution, and the thought of my brothers let loose in it turned me cold.

Julian, however, had a one-track mind. Whatever ideas he got hold of, he worked them over and over like a puppy with a slipper. "So all right," he said, "we'll set up a stall in the parking lot outside where everybody has to pass us while they've still got lots of money. And you don't have to have a license to sell. The farmer down the road has a sign up saying FRESH EGGS, and I bet he doesn't have a license."

I knew from experience that I was wasting my time arguing with him. Maybe he was right and I was prejudiced, but I just had a vague feeling of apprehension wherever Julian and Maxwell were concerned.

"Look," I said, "whatever you do, keep me out of it, okay? I'm tired of taking the blame for everything you kids do."

Julian was incensed. "We can manage fine without you," he said loftily, "but you'll have to contribute something to sell. Everyone who cares about Horse will have to; otherwise, they're phonies and don't really care about Horse at all, only about themselves!"

With this dig especially aimed at me, he took himself off indignantly, with his sidekick, Maxwell, trundling after him.

"Oh, all right!" I yelled after them angrily. "I'll crochet you some coasters, but nobody'll buy them because they never turn out right!"

I could have saved my breath. Crossing Julian was a

frustrating business. They ignored me entirely. I slid off the fence and stormed into the house where it took me ten minutes of marching up and down the sun porch to calm down again.

Oddly enough, nobody else seemed to share my apprehension. Grandma even offered to bake for them, and contribute some of her jams and preserves, while Mr. Archer started whittling miniature animals and birds out of apple, lilac and sumac branches. Margaret promised to make up posies from the garden and bake a batch of coconut candy, and Wallace offered the pick of his summer school paintings if he could remember to bring them home in time. With everyone thinking it was such a good idea, who was I to put a damper on their enthusiasm, even if it did seem to me that they had all suddenly lost their marbles? I gave up protesting, and reluctantly started on my horrible little crochet mats, which never turned out alike, and always looked to me as though a cat had been at the string.

Encouraged by all this support, the boys threw themselves into their project with even greater enthusiasm. They gave themselves two weeks and began canvassing all the local farms for contributions to their stall. Their greatest pride was the sign composed between the two of them. It was supposed to give a description of Horse's predicament, but it was so exaggerated, I couldn't believe my eyes when they showed it to me. I read it in silence until I came to the part which announced: THIS POOR HORSE HAS GIVEN HER ALL IN WILLING SERVICE TO HER MASTER AND ASKED NOTHING IN RETURN— then I felt obliged to protest.

"That poor horse has never done anything for Mr. Archer, except lean on him," I pointed out scathingly. "And she's always asking for something in return, like sugar lumps or carrots. It's too sickening for words!"

They wouldn't change a word of it, however. "It's going to get them right here!" declared Julian, thumping his chest. "Even Max and I were getting upset when we wrote it, so what do you think it's going to do to a bunch of strangers?"

"I think it's going to get you put in jail," I said. "But please yourselves. It's nothing to do with me."

It was the day of John's big show, and later that evening I went over to Holmwood Farms to see how he had fared. There were a number of cars parked outside the house, and I guessed they were having friends in after the show. That meant I wouldn't see John, but Jim would tell me all about it. He was in the stable yard, leading Queenie out of the horse trailer, as I came up. He looked up from coaxing her down the ramp.

"If you want good news, sweetheart, I'm afraid I don't have any."

"Oh, Jim!" My heart sank. "What happened?"

"Queenie wouldn't take the jumps. She kept pulling up short and shying away, so John was automatically disqualified. Well, I saw it coming."

"But I've never seen Queenie fluff a jump, Jim! She loves jumping."

Jim stroked Queenie's neck. "It wasn't her fault. It was the way John was riding her. She didn't stand a chance. His dad's been on his back too much lately. John was tight as a steel rod when he went out there today. I knew he was going to make a mess of it."

"Does that mean he won't make the Royal now?"

"I suppose he could still scrape in. He's not done too badly up to now, and it's the overall performance that counts, but he'd better not have another day like this or he'll be out for sure."

I walked beside him, while he led Queenie across the yard. The news about John depressed me as much as if it had been I who had failed. "Couldn't you talk to his father?" I begged Jim. "You could tell him to ease off the pressure a bit."

"Not me, sweetheart. I don't tell the boss how to handle his son. I only work here. Anyway, Mr. Holmes seems to think there isn't enough pressure. He thinks John doesn't take his riding seriously. He's not too happy about this afternoon, I can tell you."

"Well, couldn't you talk to his grandfather?"

"Oh, the old man thinks the same, although he tries to keep out of the arguments. It's this family-tradition thing they've got. You ought to see the trophy room they have up at the house. I'll show you one day. John's got a tough name to live up to, and I don't envy the poor kid."

At the gate of the exercise ring he handed me the leading rein and said, "How would you like to give Queenie a workout, stretch her legs a bit after being cooped up in that trailer?"

"Me?" I gaped at him. Nobody but John or Jim handled Queenie as a rule.

"Sure. Why not? Mr. Holmes has asked me to pop up to the house for a few minutes to meet this trainer from the States. You can handle her, can't you?"

I didn't know what to say. She was already saddled up ready to ride. I looked at Jim, breathless with excitement, and he laughed and said, "Sure you can. Take it easy now, and remember she's a very valuable horse. I won't be long."

I watched him go, then looked at Queenie, who looked back at me as if to say, "Well, let's get on with it." As I led her into the ring I felt as though I were treading on eggs. I mounted her and walked very, very carefully around the ring once or twice, feeling her out. She had a beautifully smooth gait. Beside her, poor old Horse would seem like a lumpy mattress.

After a while I couldn't see any harm in trying a gentle trot. She handled beautifully to the slightest pressure of my legs, and I just had to try a canter. She loved to run and it was a joy to ride her. I imagined it was me who was competing at the Royal. The empty yard became peopled with crowds, all eyes on me. I could hear the swelling murmur of applause and smell the tanbark under my feet. I must have been totally bewitched, or I would never have dreamed of trying anything so foolhardy, but suddenly I was heading Queenie right for the jump that had been left in the middle of the ring. It was only about three feet high, but I had never jumped before in my life. I wasn't even scared. I felt so instinctively right riding Queenie that it didn't even occur to me that I might fall off. Pressing my knees in tight, I moved with her, and we went up, up and over, and I was clutching her neck when we came down on the other side. I was jerked back to reality, suddenly realizing what I had done, but I wasn't sorry, only tremendously exhilarated.

And then I saw Jim. He had come back from the house and had seen me jump Queenie. My fantasy world crumbled in a heap when I saw the look on his face. I knew now that I had done something extremely childish and irresponsible and had betrayed his trust in me. He came into the ring and told me to dismount. I could not meet his eyes, I was so ashamed.

"Who taught you to jump, Joanna?"

"Nobody." My voice was almost a whisper. "I never jumped before."

There was a silence that seemed to go on forever. Then he said, "I suppose you know you could have lamed this horse, or even killed yourself. You're not even wearing a hat.

How many times have I told you to always wear your hard hat in the ring?"

I felt so small I could have crawled under a stone. Afraid of instant dismissal, I cried out in anguish, "Please don't be angry, Jim! I'll never do it again, I promise. I just felt so right on her. I seemed to know what to do. It was almost like I'd done it before. Oh, please don't tell Mr. Holmes!"

Gradually Jim's expression relaxed, but I knew I had given him a fright. "When I saw you heading for that jump, Joanna," he said, "I could feel my hair turning white. If Mr. Holmes knew about it, we'd both find ourselves unemployed."

"Oh, Jim," I said. "I'm terribly sorry! I really am."

He smiled then and put his hand on my shoulder. "I know, sweetheart. I know you didn't intend to go over that jump—you just couldn't help yourself, right?"

I nodded, tremendously relieved to be understood.

"You're a natural-born rider, Joanna, you know that? It should have been you in that show this afternoon, not John. You've got something he'll never have, not even if he practices twenty-four hours a day."

His compliment didn't make me any happier. I didn't want to be compared with John. I knew how it could end our friendship.

"Please don't tell him that," I begged Jim.

"I don't have to, sweetheart. He's going to find out for himself one of these days, along with everybody else." With this puzzling remark he dismissed me. "Take the saddle back to the tack room, and I'll cool Queenie out. I need a bit of cooling off myself after that performance."

I went as meekly as a lamb, feeling that I had won my reprieve by a hairbreadth. I opened the tack room door and almost tripped over John. He was sitting on an upturned box in the dusky twilight, staring into space.

"Hi!" I said, surprised to see him. "What are you doing here?"

He looked up at me, his expression blank. "What do I look as if I'm doing? I came here because if I go up to the house I'll be subjected to the third degree, and all I want at the moment is to be left alone. Do you mind?"

Hurt, I said timidly, "I'm sorry about this afternoon, John. Everybody has off days now and then. It doesn't mean anything."

"Oh, cut it out, Joanna!" he said sharply. "I don't need any phony pep talks. I just don't want to talk about it, okay?"

His sharp rebuke brought tears to my eyes. I turned away from him and busied myself soaping the saddle.

"You were riding Queenie, weren't you?" he said suddenly.

"How did you know?" I was afraid he would be angry about that, too. This didn't seem to be my night for getting along with people.

"Because all the other horses are either in the barn or out in the fields."

His voice was quite expressionless, as though he neither cared one way or the other, but I was sure he did. "Jim asked me if I would," I said, feebly trying to excuse myself. "He had to go up to the house, and there wasn't anybody else there. I guess he thought you were up at the house, too," I finished lamely.

"He likes you, doesn't he?"

"I guess so," I said nervously. "I like him, too, but if you're angry because of what he said the other day about me being better than you, you must know he was kidding."

103

John looked up and squinted at me. "What did you say?"

I began to repeat myself, but John cut me off short. "Oh, come off it, Joanna! You're talking nonsense. You don't think I'm jealous of you, do you?"

I hung my head, crimson in the face. "Well—well it seemed that way. You acted so funny."

John started to laugh, but it was not the funny kind of laugh we could share together. "You're crazy," he said. "I thought you knew me better than that. It was a shock to me, that's all. I didn't realize how serious you were getting. Do you think I want you to get mixed up in this sort of thing?"

"What sort of thing?" I ventured timidly.

"This cutthroat atmosphere of competition riding. I've lived with it, Joanna, ever since I can remember, and it's no fun, believe me. It warps you. You can't think beyond the next ribbon, or the next cup, or the next prize. You can't even rest on your laurels, in case somebody comes along who might be better than you are, and if you have an off day, as you very kindly call it, oh boy, you're crucified!"

I was shocked by his bitterness. I didn't know what to say.

Seeing my bewilderment, he said in a kinder tone, "You don't know what it did for me, meeting your family, Joanna. You're so normal and happy and uncomplicated. I can't bear to think of you getting into this racket. You don't belong here. Why don't you leave it alone? Why don't you know when you're well off?"

Finding my voice at last, I blurted out, "If you hate it so much, why do you do it?"

John slumped back on the box, drained of energy. "Because of my father," he said in a weary voice. "He lives through me, Joanna, so how can I back out without destroying him? Whenever I'm in the ring, it's him out there—that's why he gets so frustrated when I don't do well. He feels as though he's failed. Can you understand that?"

I nodded slowly. "I—I think so."

He looked up and gave me a sad smile. He was not angry with me anymore, but I would rather have had him angry than seen that pathetic, lost look on his face.

"What would you like to do, John?" I asked.

"Me? I don't know. Sometimes I think I'd like to be a vet. I love animals, you see. I love horses. It's not that. I used to enjoy riding, believe it or not, until I realized that for a Holmes to ride for pleasure was nothing short of sinful."

"Well, couldn't you compete and study to be a vet?" I said, trying to be helpful. "Then you could please your father and yourself."

"No way. I'm destined to go into the family stockbroking business. You see, a vet has commitments. He can't just pack up everything at a moment's notice and fly off to Europe or South America for a show. If you're in top-level riding, Joanna, and you want to stay there, you've got to be in the forefront all the time." He shot me a rueful grin. "There's no missing a show because somebody's cow happens to be sick at a crucial moment. Stockbrokers, apparently, are more dispensable."

It was nearly dark in the little tack room. A kitten jumped on John's lap, and he stroked it thoughtfully, his eyes veiled from me. My head was reeling. I couldn't believe that John could feel this way about riding, especially following my triumphant jump on Queenie. I would have thought he was the luckiest person in the world.

After a while John got up and came over to me. "You're quiet, Jo. Have I upset you, telling you all this?"

When I didn't answer at once he said, "Come on, I'll walk you home."

Together we wandered down the darkening driveway under a golden moon. The guests were still at the house. Lights were blazing and the patio lanterns were lit around the pool, but we felt very much alone and detached from it. John's hand felt for mine and I clung to it.

At our gate we faced each other for a moment. Then John said, "Thanks for listening, Jo. I feel better for having said it. I can even face the gang up at the house now, and I think I'd better, or there's going to be another almighty row tomorrow. You're a nice kid, you know that?"

I was feeling quite sensitive by this time, and I dropped my head on his shoulder because I had a feeling I was going to cry. He lifted my face gently and planted a kiss in the middle of my forehead. "Goodnight, funny face. I'll be seeing you."

"Goodnight, John," I whispered.

When he had gone I didn't go in right away. I sat on the front steps, thinking over everything he had said. I was so mixed up I didn't know whether I was happy or sad, but the kiss was wonderful. Whatever else happened, I had that to remember. At last the mosquitoes bit me half to death, and I had to give up my daydreaming and go inside.

Kitchener Market

· 11 ·

When I saw Jim the next day he informed me that he was going to take half an hour of his lunch break each day to give me a lesson.

"If I can't trust you to do what I say," he told me, "I'd better turn you into a good rider for my own peace of mind."

I started right away on a nice chestnut mare called Spirit, who was not as exciting as Queenie, but easily handled and well schooled. There were no more three-foot jumps for me. I began with the cavalletti, movable poles with the X-shaped ends, which start at ten inches, but can be built up higher into a pyramid shape by interlocking three or more, or placed parallel for spread jumps.

I made good progress and Jim was pleased with me, but I wasn't as happy as I should have been. Ever since my talk with John I had been in a confused state of mind. Part of me kept remembering the horse show, the thrill and excitement of it, and the envy I had felt for the girls who were lucky enough to compete; then I would get to wondering if I wanted only the glory of winning, of being somebody important. Much as I tried to fool myself, I couldn't deny that the prospect seemed very attractive to me. I didn't want John to despise me, and sometimes my conflicting thoughts nearly drove me crazy, until I reminded myself sternly that there was as much chance of me entering competition riding as of my going to the moon. This wasn't a very happy solution either, but at least it made me face facts.

Meanwhile, Maxwell and Julian were all ready for their big day at the market. Wallace had remembered to bring his paintings home, three of them, terrible garish things. To look at them for any long period of time you would need sunglasses. I tried to become enthusiastic about them, but Wallace must have noticed my sickly expression when he showed them to me.

"Those are real gut-stuff, man," he informed me seriously. "They should sell for a hundred dollars apiece but, seeing it's for charity, I'll let them go three for five dollars."

"That's big of you," I said, but I was thinking you would have to pay me five dollars to take them, and probably throw in a basket of strawberries as well.

The night before, the boys went to bed early because they had to be up before dawn to get Horse to the market on time, but the rest of us stayed up putting price tickets on everything. It was close to midnight by the time we got to bed, and it seemed only five minutes before the alarm went off at four-thirty, and everybody had to get up again to see Maxwell and Julian off. They were both going to ride Horse, who had a nice broad back, and Margaret, Wallace and I were going to meet them in Kitchener at six o'clock. We were taking Wallace's Volkswagen and Grandma's car, loaded up with the merchandise and trestle tables to display it on. Grandma was going to stay at home with Mr. Archer, who wasn't mobile enough to accompany us.

It was still dark when we saddled up Horse and waved the boys on their way. The scene had an unreal quality about it. Cold and sleepy, we huddled in the lighted doorway, watching the shadowy bulk of Horse with her double burden stealing down the driveway. I felt like a pioneer woman, besieged by Indians, who must send for help in the dark of night, not knowing if it would come in time. These fancies were soon dispelled when Grandma got busy at the stove, and we all filled up with pancakes, bacon and maple syrup.

Slowly the sky deepened pink over the poplars at the end of the driveway, and the redwing blackbirds and grackles took over the front lawn foraging for insects to feed their noisy youngsters, and then it was time for us to leave.

I had elected to ride with Wallace because I didn't trust Grandma's ancient car, which Margaret was driving, and I didn't want to be stranded in the middle of nowhere with a cargo of potholders, crochet mats and preserved fruits but no spare tire. Wallace was surprisingly lively for that time in the morning and gave me a lecture all the way to Kitchener on art appreciation, which I didn't appreciate at all, being half-dead. I understood now why he was usually so droopy. Anyone with that much energy at half-past five just had to be exhausted for the rest of the day.

The streets of Kitchener were almost empty of traffic, but there were pedestrians everywhere, carrying baskets and hurrying to the market, which was located in an old brick building behind the City Hall. Julian and Maxwell were sitting on the sidewalk beside Horse when we rolled up. The sight of a rather tubby horse ridden by two small boys did not cause as much of a sensation in the city as it might have done elsewhere, due to the fact that the Mennonites still used horses as their main means of transportation. In spite of my forebodings, Margaret arrived soon after us in Grandma's car. We decided to reconnoiter on foot and, leaving the cars where they were for the time being, we took a shortcut across the City Hall grounds, to the market parking lot.

"Is this it?" said Margaret, gaping.

She might well have asked, for there was not a square inch of asphalt to be seen. Julian's brilliant idea to set up his stall in the parking lot had evidently been thought of first by at least five hundred other people. All the overflow stalls from the main building were ranged around the parking area, while cars squeezed in between or parked on side streets. They were already doing a thriving business, and the place was crowded with people. Julian was leading Horse, but the sight of the crowds stopped him dead. There was hardly room for another person to edge his way through, let alone a horse of ample girth.

He looked at Maxwell, and their mouths fell open simultaneously and stayed that way. "It—it wasn't supposed to be like this," said Maxwell in a small voice. "We thought there would only be cars in the parking lot."

"Supposed!" I cried out in exasperation. "Now what? I knew we shouldn't have listened to you. I warned everybody but nobody would listen to me! You couldn't put a dime in there, let alone a stall! Now we've all worked ourselves to death, and I've crocheted those horrible mats for nothing!"

"Oh cut it out, Jo!" said Margaret, whose nerves were not as frazzled as mine. "They couldn't know. You don't have to make them feel worse than they already do. Come to think of it, you should have known, because you've been here before and they haven't."

Once again they were trying to put the blame on me, and I wasn't having it. It was true I had been to the market many years ago when I was quite small, but it seemed to me it had changed, or else I just hadn't had any reason to notice the parking lot then.

"That's not fair!" I retaliated. "Who was against the idea right from the start? Who didn't want to have anything to do with it? This is crazy! Why don't you admit I was right for once and let's all go home?"

I don't know whether Horse understood English or not, but she chose that moment to stick her muzzle into the small of my back and gave me a good shove forward, so that I nearly lost my balance.

"Good old Horse," growled Julian. "We don't want any defeatists around here."

I made up my mind that Horse and I were going to have a heart-to-heart talk when I got her on my own, but meanwhile Wallace, for the first time in his life, as far as I was concerned, began showing some sense.

"I suggest we split up and see what's going on," he suggested. "There's got to be a corner somewhere. Man, this is unreal!"

It seemed like a good idea. Leaving Margaret to guard Horse, the rest of us plunged into the crowd and elbowed our way through to the old market building. Delicious smells wafted out, reminding me that I hadn't eaten for two hours, but Wallace, Maxwell and Julian zigzagged right through to the far side without so much as a side glance at the food stalls set out to tempt us. When I stopped once, fascinated by jars of pickled pumpkin, you would have thought I had committed a major crime. Maxwell and Julian took an arm each and hustled me away like a naughty child. But when we emerged again into the west parking lot, the same scene met our eyes—stalls, people and cars all jammed together in a milling throng. Even Julian showed signs of discouragement, but suddenly Maxwell gave a shout of triumph:

"Look! Look over there!"

Attached to the main building was a small roofed annex. Two sides were completely open, and the floor of old planks looked as though it might have been used as a trapdoor at some time. We did not stop to analyze it because the only thing that caught our eye was that it was empty—beautifully, completely empty! And not only that. It occupied a perfect site, right beside the side entrance where a contant stream of people was passing.

"That's it!" screamed Julian. "You stay here and grab it, and I'll go and get Horse!"

Wallace had disappeared, but somehow we got everybody rounded up, the cars parked closer and the stall set up. Horse was pushed and pulled through the crowd and, once settled under the annex, she showed no inclination to move again. We propped up the sign in front of her, and she stood demurely chewing hay, already drawing a crowd. People stopped just to pat her and, as Julian had predicted, once they had read the sign they felt obliged to buy something.

"I wouldn't want a nice horse like that to go homeless," said one stout woman who gave us a dollar for my mats. I wished her well, but I didn't admire her taste. Even Wallace's paintings were sold in the first half-hour, which shows what kind of hypnotism Horse exerted on people.

By seven o'clock we could hardly believe it, but we had forty dollars in the kitty. We celebrated by treating ourselves to hot, paper-thin pancakes rolled up with fresh cottage cheese and jam and powdered with sugar in little squares of waxed paper. We began to relax a little. Margaret and Wallace went off to explore the market, leaving me temporarily in charge of the stall. I was quite enjoying myself now. I only wished I had crocheted more mats and had not been such a prophet of gloom.

Serenely unaware of trouble, we chatted with customers, explained about Horse and let children feed her carrots and sugar. When I saw a policeman in the crowd, towering head and shoulders above everybody else, I wasn't particularly worried, until I noticed that he seemed to have an abnormal interest in us and our stall. It wasn't Horse he was staring at, like the other people, just Julian, Maxwell and me, and something about the way he was looking at us sent off warning signals in my brain. Through long experience I knew that the Longfellow bad luck was about to strike again. Cowardly though it was, I slunk out of sight behind Horse, making myself as scarce as possible. If there was going to be trouble, I absolutely refused to take the blame again. Let Julian and Maxwell be responsible for their own brilliant ideas for a change.

The policeman pushed his way through the crowd to our stall. Maxwell, busy with serving, hadn't noticed him yet. Then, looking up and saying "Next please," he met the eyes of the law. He gulped and paled, but rallied bravely. Thrusting a bottle of preserved plums at the policeman, he said staunchly, "Fresh out of the garden, sir. Only forty cents a jar. It's a real steal!"

I flinched at Maxwell's unfortunate choice of words. Peering around Horse's tail, I saw the policeman ignore the plums and lean gravely over Maxwell. "Do you have a license to sell here, young fellow?" he asked politely.

At the sight of six foot, four inches of policeman

towering over him, Maxwell's bravado collapsed, and it was Julian who finally said, in a voice which quavered slightly, "But we're not in the market, sir. We're in the parking lot."

"Well, that doesn't make any difference," the policeman told him. "You're still selling at the market even if you're outside the building, but as a matter of fact you're not even on the parking lot. You're on the weigh scale."

"The weigh scale?" Julian looked down at the boards under his feet, and his face turned pale. I remembered now that the floor had seemed bouncy as we walked back and forth across it. I cursed myself for being such an idiot. Of course, what we had thought was a trapdoor was the scale that the trucks drove onto, through the open ends of the structure, to have their loads checked! That explained why it had been empty when we found it. It had also served to make us very conspicuous. If our stall had been lost among all the others, it was quite possible the policeman wouldn't have noticed anything fishy about us.

An interested knot of people had gathered around us. A jolly, round-faced farmer pleaded with the policeman. "Don't be too hard on the young'uns, officer. They're doing it for their horse. You can read it all there—see? I think it's a grand thing to be doing."

There were murmurs of assent from the crowd, which seemed to be on our side. The policeman turned his attention to Horse and read the sign, but he didn't melt as everybody else had done. Instead, he ordered the disruptive crowd to move away from the stall and took Julian and Maxwell aside. Then he saw me cowering behind Horse. "Are you in on this?" he asked.

I came forward reluctantly. "I'm their sister," I said.

"They honestly didn't mean any harm. Even our grandmother thought it was all right."

"And we really do need the money for Horse," piped up Maxwell, getting his courage back. "If she doesn't have a barn this winter she'll have nowhere to go, and she'll end up at the glue factory for sure, then her old master will die of grief."

I stepped on Maxwell's toe hard. There was such a thing as laying it on too thick.

Julian said in a hollow voice, "What are you going to do with us? Send us to jail?"

The policeman pursed his lips and scratched his nose. He seemed to be making a great show out of thinking. "No-o," he said at last, drawing out the word, "I don't think you'll be sent to jail. But you could be fined for selling without a license and without the permission of the market authorities. Also for blocking a public utility."

"All that?" Maxwell and Julian turned pale.

"Could we use the money we've made to pay the fines?" asked Julian, practical as always even in times of stress.

Maxwell objected strongly to that. "Then what would Horse do? She wouldn't get her barn!" He screwed up his face in agonized thought and came up with the brilliant idea. "Maybe we could have another stall to pay our fines," he said.

Between them I didn't think they were making the situation any better. Seen close up, the policeman had quite a nice face. I decided to put ourselves at his mercy and explain everything to him.

When I had finished, the policeman turned and looked Horse up and down as though he had just become aware of her presence. I closed my eyes and prayed silently and fervently that Horse would turn on her charm to its full extent, and not nip him or do something dreadful. She did not let us down. Giving a little whicker, she reached her velvety nose forward to nuzzle his breast pocket, where she was used to people keeping lumps of sugar. I'll swear she batted her eyelashes at him. Then came her crowning achievement. She took a step forward and leaned on him.

The policeman looked embarrassed but flattered. He was not to know, of course, that she leaned on everybody. "She's a nice old girl, all right," he said, removing his holster from between Horse's teeth. "I can see why you want to keep her."

He turned back to where we were standing, stiff and miserable in a row behind him. He put his notebook back in his pocket and studied us thoughtfully. "Now let me see," he said. "It takes me about half an hour to make a tour of the marketplace. How long do you think it would take you to pack up all this and disappear?"

Catching on, we all chorused gleefully together, "Twenty-five minutes!"

"Good! Then I haven't seen you. When I come back I want to see this weigh scale quite empty, you understand? No litter, or anything. Okay?"

"Yes, sir!" we cried joyously. Maxwell was already shoveling the remaining jams and preserves into a box under the table.

"And," said the policeman, giving me a wink, "I'll take a couple of those bottled plums." He fished in his pocket for a dollar and said, "Keep the change. Buy the horse an apple for me."

We gave him the biggest and best plums we could find.

"Wow!" said Maxwell in awe, when he had gone. "If

the kids ever say anything bad about the police again, I'll bust their teeth in!"

"He was fantastic!" I agreed fervently. "If he'd have me, I'd marry him!"

We had made sixty-seven dollars and ten cents, and had sold about three-quarters of our stuff, so what if we did have to pack up a little early? We had done much better than we had dared to hope, and had escaped juvenile court in the bargain. It was an occasion for rejoicing. By the time Wallace and Margaret returned, we had dismantled everything and were ready to go. In a few terse sentences we explained to them what had happened, and they helped us get the stuff back to the cars. In twenty minutes we had everything packed away, and Horse saddled up. I had never seen Wallace move so fast in my life. We looked at each other in silence; then suddenly we were all laughing and whooping it up on the pavement.

"Sixty-seven dollars!" I cried excitedly. "That ought to buy enough lumber to build the framework for a very small barn, and Mr. Archer said we could salvage the rest from the big barn. So we did it!"

"Whoopee!" cried Maxwell. "Let's hurry home and tell Mr. Archer and Gran!"

They wouldn't stop, not even when somebody suggested going for a soda, they were so eager to be the bearers of good tidings. We helped them up on Horse, and watched them go, a perky little pair astride Horse's comfortable bulk. Even if I had had the chance, I wouldn't have traded her for Queenie at that moment. She might fall short when it came to looks and grace, but what other horse could charm a policeman and earn the money for its own barn without exerting a muscle? She was a very special horse, all right.

The rest of us went into a snack bar and treated

ourselves to ice cream because we thought we deserved it. While we were there, Wallace made the supreme effort, and actually promised to help us build the barn. Knowing his aversion to work of any kind, I was touched.

"That's great, Wallace," I said. "Welcome to the working classes."

He grinned at me and I grinned back, all our differences forgotten.

It was a pleasant drive home. We skipped the highway and took maple-shaded side lanes where whitewashed Mennonite homesteads drowsed in the sunshine, and smart black buggies rolling home from market churned up the dust under the horses' flying hooves. We killed time purposely, not wanting to steal the boys' thunder by arriving home first. It was lunchtime when we finally pulled in the driveway. There was a little English-model car parked in front of us. Margaret and I jumped out of our respective cars and stared at each other; then we let out a screech and dashed into the house.

"They're home!" I cried out over my shoulder to Wallace, who must have thought we had flipped our lids. "Our parents are home!"

Mother was just the same, laughing with delight to see us, but I hardly knew Father because of his huge, bushy red beard. As he enveloped me in his whiskery embrace, he said, "Well, my Jo, Grandma's been telling me you've become quite a horsewoman while we've been away."

I nodded, giggling as his beard tickled my nose. "You'll just have to shave it off, Daddy. Gee, it's good to see you again!"

I meant it, I really did, but just underneath my happiness a hateful little voice was saying, "This is the end, Joanna— the end of Horse, of Queenie, of riding every day, the end of

118

John. Back to the hateful city and shuffling around, and not belonging anywhere anymore."

I buried my face in my father's tweedy shoulder, desperately trying to stifle that voice. Reunions were supposed to be happy times, and I didn't want to spoil their homecoming by bursting into tears.

John Takes Off

· 12 ·

There were two reasons why my parents had arrived home unexpectedly. My father had come to the end of his grant money, and he had been offered a job doing a series of television scripts in Toronto. The job offer had come at an opportune time and presented a challenge to my father, who immediately tired of Mexico and dashed home. That was the way he operated. There was so much news to exchange that, for a couple of days, we seemed to spend all our time talking. Even poor old Horse was somewhat neglected, but Mr. Archer had assured us that we would be able to come up with some sort of barn for sixty-seven dollars plus scrap wood from the old barn. So her future was taken care of.

Ours was more hazy. After the first excitement had worn off, Father called a conference in the sleeping porch, which he and Mother had taken over from the boys, who now slept temporarily in a tent in the backyard. Father presided over the conference, while we sprawled over the beds eating pretzels and horsing around.

"All right!" boomed out Father. "If you can just manage to keep your voices down to a dull roar, we'll call this meeting to order."

We subsided into silence, punctuated only by crunching noises, and Father continued, "Now that your mother and I are back, it is out of the question to go on imposing on the hospitality of your grandmother any longer."

"Why is it?" demanded Maxwell.

"Because you may like living like a sardine, Maxwell, but I personally find it extremely inconvenient to line up for two to three hours every time I wish to go to the bathroom. Also, as you know, I shall be working in Toronto for the next six months or so, and I don't relish commuting sixty miles a day for the privilege of living in a house which, at times, resembles Grand Central Station on a holiday weekend. Does that answer your question?"

"No," said Maxwell. "I like it here."

"So do I," said Julian.

"So do I," I said. "Besides, we have to build the barn."

Father snorted. "You're developing impossibly bucolic tastes. You're turning into a bunch of country bumpkins. Don't you sometimes crave a little culture—a theater perhaps, or an art gallery, or a museum?"

"No," we said in chorus.

"All right, that's your affair, but think of your grandmother. Has it ever occurred to you that she might like to have her household back to normal again?"

We couldn't answer that, and Father seized on our silence as proof positive. "Aha, so you do have a guilty conscience there, I see! The fact remains, my dear offspring, that I must start hunting for a place to live shortly and, if you have any preferences as to where you want to be, reasonably close to the city, I am open to suggestions."

"We don't want to live in the city," persisted Maxwell doggedly, "anywhere!"

Father was disgusted with us. "I can see I'm wasting my time trying to treat you like adults. In future I shall not seek your cooperation. Your mother and I will go looking tomorrow, and you will live where we choose to live, and there will be no squawking—is that clear?"

I stared at him in dismay. "Tomorrow!" I cried. "Oh, Daddy, not so soon! What about my riding?" I had known all along that we would have to go someday, but this was too sudden. I was not prepared for it.

"Oh, come now, Joanna," said Father, fast losing his patience. "Don't look so tragic. They don't have a monopoly on horses here. You can find a riding stable near the city and have lessons, if that's what you want."

I knew he was being generous, and I hadn't the heart to say anything even though I knew how it would be. I would get my lessons every Saturday for a while until the bills started to pile up. Then I would be forced to skip a lesson here and there until finally the whole thing became a farce. But how could I say this to my father, who always meant so well? He had a knack of convincing himself that everything he wanted to do he did for our benefit, and he would have been genuinely hurt if someone had told him otherwise.

Mother looked at me compassionately, reading my thoughts. She knew Father even better than I did, having lived with him longer. Trying to cushion the shock of departure for me, she coaxed him: "Do you have to be in such a hurry, dear? There's still almost a month before school starts, and I'd like a little break before setting up house again. Besides, the children really ought to build that barn, since they went to all that trouble to earn the money. I'm really quite enjoying it here with Mother."

Father looked at her as though she had gone mad, but he capitulated, writing her off with us as past redemption. "Very well, my dear, if you want to vegetate in these backwoods for another month, be my guest. However, I have to go into the city tomorrow for a meeting, so I shall spend a few days in a civilized hotel and look around for somewhere to live." He hauled his bulk out of the chair and gave us all a pitying look. "What a strange lot of offspring I have spawned, and you were all so promising when you were small."

This was too much for Margaret, who immediately protested that she didn't mind living in the city at all; in fact, she loved it, but that was only because Wallace was going back to college in September. She was the only one who would gain anything by moving.

"Traitor!" I hissed at her.

She reddened and skulked out of the room after Father. Left alone with us, Mother lifted her hands helplessly.

"I did what I could, children, but you must admit we are too crowded here. How would you ever get any homework done, when school started? And the boys can't sleep in a tent all winter. That's silly."

I felt too hollow inside to care much anymore. "Well," I said dismally, "I suppose I'd better go and tell Jim he can have his lunch hours back again, because I won't be riding anymore."

I was overflowing with self-pity as I walked into the tack room. Jim, taking one look at me, said, "Good gracious me, what's the matter with you, sweetheart?"

"I won't be needing any more lessons," I blurted out. "My father's going to take us all back to the city in September." I had meant to be stoical about the whole thing, but my voice broke down and the next thing I was sobbing uncontrollably. Jim came over and let me cry on his shoulder. He smelled of horses and dust and earth, the smell of the stables that I had come to love. After I had calmed down a bit he said gently, "You've still got four weeks, sweetheart. We can get in a lot of lessons in four weeks."

"But what for?" I cried out in anguish. "It's not worth bothering with if I'm going to have to give up riding!"

Jim stood back and looked at me thoughtfully. "I don't think you mean that," he said.

"I do!" I protested. "I can't see any point in it."

Jim shrugged. "Well, if that's the way you feel, you're right. There isn't any point. So—I'll see you around." He turned and walked out of the tack room, leaving me alone.

I was stunned out of my self-pity. I couldn't believe he would dismiss me so casually after all the time he had spent coaching me. Angrily, I ran after him. "Why did you bother with me at all?" I accused him. "If you didn't think I was worth it, why did you give me lessons?"

I was too upset to be rational. Jim looked at me, his face grave and kind. "Sweetheart, if you want pity, you've come to the wrong person. I've no time for quitters. You've had one setback, and you're ready to drop everything. I thought you had more spirit than that. Why, when I first knew you, I think you'd have given your right arm to have one lesson. Now you can have a whole month, and that's not enough for you. Well, let me tell you something, sweetheart, nobody knows what's going to happen tomorrow. John's father didn't know he was going to lose a leg during the war and would never ride again, but I doubt if he regrets all the time he spent training. It was probably the happiest time in his life. You make the most of what you can get in this life, sweetheart, when you can get it. If everybody started thinking about what might happen next month or next year, they'd be too scared to do anything."

It was the longest speech I had ever heard Jim make, and I was ashamed of myself. He had been so good to me, and I was being so ungrateful. He had every right to ditch me right then and there, but now I knew that a month of riding was far, far better than no riding at all and I was terribly afraid that I had forfeited it.

Jim, looking at me quizzically, said, "You want to learn to ride well, don't you?"

"Oh, yes!" I cried eagerly. "I love riding, I really do, Jim! I know I'm not all that good yet, but that time I jumped on Queenie, it was like flying. I felt I had wings, like I was part of her, you know what I mean? I'd like to feel that way again, just once."

Jim smiled and put his arm around my shoulder. "And so you shall, sweetheart, I promise you. We'll make a good rider out of you before September, and we'll let the future take care of itself, shall we? Now, how about getting Spirit tacked up? We've already wasted ten minutes."

I didn't waste another second, and after that I carried on with my daily lessons, but now I worked harder than ever before. It was true you could never foresee what was going to happen. If anyone had told me four months ago that I would be riding at Holmwood Farms and have John Holmes for a friend, I would have told them they were crazy.

We had the barn to think about, too. Somehow we had to get it built before September, and it took priority over everything else. Mr. Archer drew up some plans, and we bought what lumber we could afford and raided the old barn for the rest. Wallace began bringing home fellow students from the art school to help, and they were such a merry lot it was not like work at all. We roasted corn and frankfurters to feed the hungry workers, and there was always somebody with a guitar to make music. If the work did not always progress as quickly as it might have, that was all to the good, because we were having so much fun we wanted to spin it out as long as possible.

Father came home on Saturday night into the middle of this merriment. I thought he would have a fit when he saw the chaos in the backyard. Six of the boys had formed a rock group, and the noise was deafening. Wallace was on the roof of the old barn with Julian and Maxwell, flinging shingles down to a group of squealing girls who were gathering them up into piles, and Margaret was doing her version of a tribal war dance with a handsome, bearded student who wore beads. In the middle of all this Mother and Grandma scuttled back and forth between kitchen and yard with armfuls of corn and pans of gingerbread.

I watched Father nervously as he stood on the back porch and surveyed the scene below him. Before he had time to explode, Mother thrust an opened bottle of beer in his hand, gave him a smile and a quick kiss, then left him to his own devices. Before long his writer's curiosity took over, and he was mingling with the young people trying to find out their views on everything. After a while, and a few more beers, he became quite expansive and even had a go on the drums, while twenty-four art students clapped their hands and egged him on. Then Mr. Archer gave him a hammer and put him to work on the frame of the new barn. The hammering appealed to him. He said it got rid of his frustrations. He became so adept at it that we couldn't stop him.

"Daddy, go easy!" I appealed to him. "We don't want to finish the barn tonight. We want to make it last until September."

He took a handful of nails from his teeth, waved the hammer in a grand gesture and declared, "That's all right, chicken. When this is done, we'll build a tool shed."

"Grandma doesn't have any tools, Daddy," I sighed.

He was astonished. "What? No tools? Everybody should have tools. We'll get her some." He gave me a broad wink and went back to his hammering.

"I thought you didn't like madhouses," I said.

"Ah, but this is organized madness, chicken," he informed me. "It is disorganized insanity which I find very hard on the nerves. Now leave me alone, there's a good girl. I find this manual work very soothing. I might even take up carpentry."

So that was my father, unpredictable as always. John came over later. I hadn't seen much of him since his failure in the Class A show. He was training harder than ever and had gained another red ribbon, which had put him back in the running for the Royal in October, but he was more withdrawn than before, and he didn't seem happy.

We strolled away from the others where we could talk, and he said to me, "I wish October was over, Jo. It's like a sword hanging over my head."

"You'll do all right," I told him. "You worry too much."

"I didn't do all right last year. I made a hell of a mess of it. I couldn't face that again, not with everybody expecting so much of me. I wish I'd never been born a Holmes sometimes. How easy life would be if I'd just been plain John Smith."

I hated to hear him talk like that. I felt so inadequate when I tried to cheer him up. "You've had an extra year's training since last year," I reminded him. "And you're good, John, you know you are. If you'd just get over this hangup you have, always being afraid you're going to fail. You should be like Wallace and think beautiful."

He laughed and squeezed my hand. "Maybe you're right. At least he always seems to get what he wants. Anyway, the boss says three days a week training from now until October, so I'll be down every Thursday from now on. Did your father find a place to live yet?"

At the mention of that, my own spirits plummeted. "He's got several lined up," I said miserably. "It's just a question of making up his mind."

"We are a couple of cheerful Charlies, aren't we?" said John. "Anyway, I'll tell you what—if I ever survive this wretched show I'll pick you up some evening and we'll have a night on the town. We'll do exactly what we want to do without anybody on our backs. Would you like that?"

"Oh," I said, "I'd love it."

"Then it's a date, Jo. Put it in your little black book."

He had to go home soon after that, because his father had forbidden late nights, but he left me walking on air. I knew that John liked me here on the farm, where fate had thrown us together and there wasn't any competition, but it had never in my wildest dreams occurred to me that he would look me up in Toronto, where he could have his pick of the most gorgeous girls on the campus. When I went to bed that night I was so happy that the loss of my riding career no longer seemed like the end of the world. All the same I couldn't help thinking how ironic life could be at times. I should have been John, and he should have been me, and then neither of us would have had any problems at all.

Father had started his script-writing job and was living in a hotel for the time being. He came home weekends, and early Saturday morning he rolled up just as a truck drew into our driveway and deposited a load of new lumber in our backyard. We all ran out, convinced there had been some mistake, but Father was there before us.

"It's for the tool shed," he informed us. "This is my own project. I don't want to spoil the fun for you youngsters, but after a week of working with a bunch of prima donnas, building something with my own hands will be excellent therapy for nervous tension."

There must have been at least a hundred dollars' worth of wood on the lawn, more than we had bought for the whole barn. I groaned inwardly, seeing my last hopes of riding lessons in the city disappearing fast.

Nothing surprised Mother anymore. She merely said with resignation, "Well, I hope you can build it in two weekends, dear, because that's all the time we have left here. You'll have to find something else for your nervous tension when we're living in the city unless you intend to build a tool shed on the balcony."

Father, happy as a child with his pile of wood, was undismayed. "Time enough to cross our bridges when we come to them," he informed us benevolently. "Maybe I'll take up jogging."

It was no use reasoning with him, so we went back inside to prepare for the influx of hungry students that we expected later on. After lunch, everybody rested except Julian and Maxwell, who had decided that Horse must learn to jump, an idea which Horse did not share. It was a frustrating experience and, after watching them for a while through the kitchen window, I got myself a book and settled down to read while the house was quiet.

A little later John came in. He didn't bother to knock anymore. It was a very hot day, and he looked exhausted. "I've had it," he said. "I've been working out since nine o'clock, so I figure I've earned a rest. You wouldn't happen to have something nice and cool to drink, would you, Jo?"

I made him a tall, fizzy lemon soda, and he told me that I

was an absolutely marvelous girl, and that he was going to lock me up so no one else could get me. I loved it when he talked like that, even though he was only teasing. We were sitting companionably drinking our sodas when a rap came on the door. Opening it, I found Jim standing there apologetically.

"Sorry to bother you, sweetheart, but is John there? His dad's looking for him."

John had got up and stood behind me. "What does he want, Jim?" he asked in a tight voice.

"He'd like to see how your jumping's coming along. He's waiting up at the barn."

A slow flush spread over John's face. He said, barely controlling his anger, "Did you tell him how hard I've been working for the past three days? Is it too much to expect that I can have just half an hour off to myself? I suppose he saw me come over here. That's what's irking him, isn't it?"

Poor Jim looked uncomfortable. It was a ticklish situation acting as go-between for John and his father. "I told him you'd really been sweating it out this morning, kid, and that I didn't think a bit of relaxation would hurt you, but he says there'll be plenty of time for fun and games after the Royal." Jim shrugged helplessly. "What else could I say?"

"Nothing, Jim, nothing." I could tell that John was furious. Without even saying good-bye to me, or finishing his soda, he strode out of the door, almost pushing Jim aside. Jim and I looked at each other, not knowing what to say.

"Well, sweetheart," said Jim sadly, "I'd better get back there, too, and see if I can smooth things over."

I didn't envy him his task, but there was no point in worrying about it. Luckily, I had Saturday night festivities to look forward to. They were always fun, and nobody could stay gloomy long in such an atmosphere. Father was good enough to leave the barn-building to us this time, and started on his tool shed. He enjoyed himself so much that he worked on it all day Sunday and had to be forced to come in to meals. It looked a bit lopsided to me, but I was no expert. I didn't see John again that weekend, but I hadn't expected to, with his father there to keep an eye on him.

The Holmes family always went back to the city on Monday mornings, so it was quite a shock to me, when I went over for my midday lesson, to find John's father and old Mr. Holmes in the tack room talking to Jim. Flustered, I turned back to the door, intending to leave, in case I was intruding, but old Mr. Holmes called after me, "Just a minute, Joanna. You're quite friendly with John, aren't you?"

I nodded, feeling my heart thumping. They were all looking at me so strangely.

"When did you see him last?"

I couldn't grasp what was going on. "Last Saturday when Jim came to get him," I said. "I haven't seen him since."

"Did he say anything to you about leaving?"

"Leaving?" I stared at him in utter dismay. I didn't know what they were talking about.

Jim saw my confusion and thought he had better explain. "He's gone, Joanna. He must have packed up and left in the night. We were wondering if you knew anything about it."

Exciting News

· 13 ·

I should have been more prepared than I was, but the news came as a shock to me. I remember sitting down on an upturned box, because my legs suddenly felt weak, and old Mr. Holmes pulling up a chair in front of me. His face was worried but kind.

"Try and remember, Joanna. Didn't he say anything at all to you that might give us a hint as to where he's gone?"

I shook my head helplessly. I didn't believe John had planned this. I think he had been driven to the limit and something inside him had finally snapped. "Maybe he's staying with friends," I suggested lamely.

"No. We've phoned everywhere. Nobody's seen him. All he left was a note saying he was tired of being dependent and was going to plan his own future from now on. I don't have to tell you what a terrible shock this is to us, Joanna. We had such great hopes for him, and he's all we have, his father and I."

I stole a timid look at John's father. I thought he had aged overnight. "We've given that boy everything, everything he's ever needed," he said bitterly, "and this is how he repays us."

I had to feel sorry for him, but I had to be loyal to John, too. I remembered the times I had seen John in torment, torn between his own wishes and his unwillingness to hurt his father.

I said timidly, because I was still very much in awe of Mr. Holmes, "I don't think John planned to run away. I just don't think he felt he could live up to what you expected of him. He didn't really care for competition riding at all, but he knew you did and he was terribly afraid of letting you down. That's all he ever talked about."

Mr. Holmes turned, and his eyes seemed to bore right through me. "And wouldn't you call this letting me down?" he said, his voice icy. "I would rather he failed honorably than ran away like a coward."

That was too much for me. I blurted out without thinking, "That's not fair! You never tried to understand him. He didn't want to ride, he didn't want to go into your business, he wanted to be a vet, but he was prepared to give that all up for you, and all you could do was criticize him all the time. You never praised him or encouraged him. No wonder he left!"

My audacity left me shaking in my shoes, but I wasn't sorry I had said it. Somebody had to tell him, and there seemed to be nobody on John's side except me.

I startled Mr. Holmes, who was obviously not used to being answered back by his very minor employees, even if I had been a friend of John's. I saw a muscle under his eye twitch, and I had the feeling that he was barely controlling his anger and was holding me responsible for being a bad influence on John. Luckily, Jim intervened just then.

"There's something in what she says, sir. He's been really down lately, especially about the Royal coming up. It preyed on his mind. He was afraid he was going to let you down again, and he couldn't face it. But he did try hard. I think he worked himself up into such a nervous state, something just had to crack."

"Why didn't you tell us this before?" demanded old Mr. Holmes.

"Well, begging your pardon, sir, I have tried to get you to ease up on him a bit, but even so it would probably have come to this sooner or later. John likes riding but he just hasn't got that extra little spark, that something that makes champions. Joanna here, now, she's got it. What would be punishment for John would be a challenge for her. It's not something you can force—it's something you're born with."

It was nice of Jim to plug me, but neither of them were interested in me at that moment. In fact, I am sure John's father resented my being there at all.

Old Mr. Holmes put his hand on Jim's shoulder and said, in a preoccupied voice, "Thanks, Jim. I wish we could have talked about this sooner, but don't blame yourself. We'd better get back to the house in case we hear anything. Now that we know why he went, we might be able to straighten things out, if we could only find out where he is."

John's father didn't look at me as he went out. He seemed lost in a tragic world of his own, and I wished now that I hadn't been so blunt with him. The truth was sometimes too unkind to bear. I wished I could have apologized to him, but I knew it wouldn't help. He had forgotten me already. I was nobody to him.

Jim and I were left alone in the tack room. He came and sat down beside me. "He'll be all right," he said, patting my hand, thinking no doubt that my woeful face was for John, which it partly was. "It'll make a man out of him, learning to stand on his own two feet. He won't be the first one to have done it and come out okay. He should have done it long ago, to my way of thinking."

But I couldn't forget the look on Mr. Holmes's face. It haunted me. "What will his father do?" I said, biting my lip. "John was all he lived for. Did you see the way he looked when he went out, almost as if John had died or something?" Strangely enough it was Mr. Holmes I was feeling sorry for now, more than for John. I closed my eyes tight, but the tears squeezed out of the lids. "I didn't want to hurt him like that!" I cried out in anguish. "I didn't want to hurt anybody. I just thought it was best that he knew."

"And it was best, sweetheart, so don't upset yourself about it." Dear, kind Jim put his arm around my shoulders, and I needed comfort badly just then. "Sure you feel sorry for him, and so do I, but no one can live their life through somebody else. John's done him a good turn without knowing it. The pride of the Holmeses has become an obsession with him. It's sort of a sickness. John could never place second or third—that was as bad as losing. He had to be first all the time. Pride comes before a fall, they say, and there never was a truer word spoken. For all you beat your head against a wall, life has a funny way of sorting things out."

"But why does somebody always have to get hurt?" I

said miserably. It was not a nice sight to see a proud man crumple up, his dreams in ruins. "He doesn't have anything left now that John's gone."

Jim smiled to himself. "I wouldn't call all this nothing, sweetheart."

"Oh, material things!" I said scornfully. "They don't make you happy."

"Neither does false pride or hankering after glory for its own sake. There's more to life than that, and the sooner a person finds that out the better for him."

I looked at him with new eyes. "Then you agree with John? You think competition riding is bad?"

"Oh, bless you, no!" Jim looked shocked at the idea. "Life would be pretty dull without competition. How else could you measure your progress in anything without some sort of competition? It's healthy enough until winning becomes an obsession. Then it becomes dangerous. When you can't lose graciously and admit that someone is better than you are, then you'd better quit. Don't take too much notice of anything John told you. He's been under a lot of strain this last year. There's nothing wrong with competing, and nothing wrong with feeling proud of yourself if you win, either, so long as you never lose your perspective. You've got to learn to handle success as well as failure, and I think you could, sweetheart. I think you're the stuff that champions are made of, so don't let anything John said worry you."

Nobody could be told such a thing without bucking up considerably, but one thing was worrying me. "Will Mr. Holmes want me to work here now?" I asked anxiously. "I mean, I was rather rude to him and I know I don't have much time left, but I do want to learn everything I can for as long as I can."

"That's the spirit," said Jim, his eyes twinkling. "Anyway, old Mr. Holmes is the boss when it comes to hiring people, and somebody has to exercise Queenie now John's gone."

"Queenie!" I gasped. "You mean—?"

In answer, Jim took Queenie's saddle off the peg and dumped it over my arm. "Go and saddle her up. I'll be out to give you a lesson in just a minute."

So I rode Queenie again, and jumped the three-foot fence under Jim's supervision and, if it hadn't been for worrying over John and his father, I think I would have been the happiest girl in the world. Queenie's gait was effortless, responding to my slightest touch, and her jumping so smooth and stretched and full of controlled power. I was even reconciled to going back to the city, for to have ridden and jumped on Queenie was to have lived gloriously, and nobody could ever take the memory of it away from me.

As the days passed I held on to the rather wistful hope that John might call me, but I knew I was attaching too much importance to our brief relationship. Away from the atmosphere of his home, where my family had helped relieve the tension, he would have no more need for me. Still, whenever the phone rang, I raced to answer it. Once it was Father calling from the city. He had finally managed to sublet a place for eight months from an actor friend who was going abroad.

"You'll love it, chicken!" he told me enthusiastically. "Eighteen floors up and you can see right over the lake—a tremendous view! And there's a swimming pool and sauna in the basement. You'll be able to have your chums over to swim. Didn't I tell you to trust your old father?"

"Yes, Daddy," I said dutifully, but I already hated it. If it had looked out over a garbage dump, it would have been all the same to me.

I rode Queenie every day and tried to close my eyes to the fact that time was running out for me and my days at Holmwood Farms were numbered. Maxwell and Julian had become resigned. They had become spoiled by the use of the Holmeses' pool, so the fact that our new home had its own pool helped. It would be terrible leaving Horse, but they knew they would see her occasionally at Christmas and other holidays, so they didn't have as much to lose as I had.

The last weekend at Grandma's arrived, and with it Father, eager to finish his tool shed. He had really done quite a presentable job for a beginner. As I crossed the yard on my way to Holmwood Farms, he called out to me gaily, "How does that look, chicken?"

I managed to give him a sickly smile. "Lovely, Daddy," I said. I knew he couldn't help being the way he was, anymore than I could, but the knowledge wasn't very comforting at that moment.

Tonight we were going to have the grand opening of the new barn, and it was to be a very special farewell party for all the art students and for us, too. Everybody would be splitting up and going their own way. I wished John could have been there to share it with me. I remembered how he had promised to look me up in the city, but that seemed unlikely now.

I stopped to give some clover to Horse, who had come loping over to greet me as I passed her field. I rubbed her velvety nose and buried my face in her tangled mane. "I wish I could change places with you," I whispered in her ear, and she rolled her big brown eyes in sympathy. But I had work to do, and I couldn't spend my last Saturday moping.

I ran across the ripening fields to the stables. Goldenrod and fall asters glorified the hedgerows, and birds flocked and chattered in rows on the telephone wires. Like me, next week they would be gone.

I went into the big barn and picked up a bucket and spade for mucking out. Down at the far end Mr. Holmes was talking to Jim. I ducked quickly into the first empty stall and began shoveling furiously, hoping he hadn't seen me. I didn't think I would be very popular with him, so my scalp prickled ominously when I heard him call out curtly, "Joanna, come here a minute, will you?"

I put down my shovel and slunk nervously down the rows of stalls. I could feel him looking at me as I approached, and I couldn't meet his eyes.

"Never mind the cleaning out," he said brusquely. "I want to see you ride."

I reacted like a moron, gaping at him and stuttering, "B-but I'm supposed to clean out on Saturdays. That's what I get paid for." As if he didn't know that! I was too confused to think straight.

"You'll get paid," he said impatiently. "Go and saddle up Queenie and take her into the ring."

I did as I was told, but I sensed a trap somewhere. Was he about to accuse me of ruining Queenie by my clumsy riding, to pay me back for the way I had talked to him? I couldn't think of any other reason. I was so nervous, it took me twice as long to get her bridle on than it usually did, and then the saddle girth got twisted. I was all thumbs and nearly in tears when I finally rode her out to the ringside where Mr. Holmes and Jim awaited me.

"All right," barked out Mr. Holmes. "Walk her around a couple of times. Then trot!"

I obeyed, but I felt like the sack of potatoes that Julian had called me the first time I had ridden Horse. I was so taut that Queenie felt it and acted up. It was terrible. After a minute, Jim stepped into the ring and caught hold of her bridle. "Relax, Joanna," he said gently. "Nobody's going to eat you. Just pretend there's nobody here but you and Queenie. If you freeze up in front of us, what are you going to do at the Royal?"

What are you going to do at the Royal? I didn't understand what Jim was talking about, but the words burned into my brain, opening up possibilities undreamed of. I was suddenly conscious of Queenie beneath me, powerful and strong, holding in all that glorious speed and grace that only I could release. Under my old sweater, my heart was thumping. I gave Jim a tremulous smile, and he said, "That's better. Off you go now, and remember there's no one here but you and Queenie."

He tapped her lightly on the flank with his crop and we started around again, but this time it was different because I was in control. Automatically I obeyed the orders that Mr. Holmes fired at me, but I was alone with Queenie, just the two of us in some wonderful dream world where there was no unhappiness, no disappointment, and no shattered hopes. When it came to jumping, I started low and went on progressively until I had cleared five feet, six inches higher than I had ever tackled before. Queenie took the jumps in her wonderful, flowing stride. I felt bewitched, and I think I must have been. When Mr. Holmes ordered me to dismount, I seemed to fall out of the sky on to solid ground.

Jim was grinning all over his homely face. "Great, kid, great!" he said, for my ears alone. "Well, what do you think, sir?" he said to Mr. Holmes, whose expression as he watched me was quite inscrutable.

Holding my breath, I waited for his answer. I had a

horrible feeling that, although he was looking at me, he was seeing John. My heart sank when he turned away and leaned on the fence without saying anything. I felt dismissed. I wanted to creep away and hide, which I probably would have done if Jim didn't have his hand on my shoulder, keeping me there.

At last Mr. Holmes said, without turning around, "How would you like to ride Queenie in the Royal next year?"

"*Me?*" My knees had started to tremble. I looked at Jim, speechless, and he was beaming at me, as though he had known all along that this would happen.

"Well?" Mr. Holmes turned sharply and pinned me under his direct gaze. "I think I could make something of you if you're willing to work hard—and I mean hard. If I take you on I mean business, Joanna. Let's get that straight from the beginning."

Suddenly my elation toppled dizzily and left me in despair. "But I'm leaving! I won't be here!" I cried out in my misery. "My father's taking us back to Toronto next week."

Mr. Holmes brushed this aside as though it were too trivial an item to bother him with. "You can stay with your grandmother, can't you? You're old enough now to be on your own. I'll talk to your father. Is he over there this weekend?"

I nodded, still in a state of shock.

"Tell him I'll be over later, then, to have a talk with him."

He was not a man to let anything stand in his way, once he had made up his mind, but I still couldn't believe this was happening to me—plain Joanna Longfellow, who six months ago hardly knew one end of a horse from another.

"But—why me?" I asked in little more than a whisper.

"Why not you? You have the potential, and Jim tells me you're very keen and you're a good worker. That's all I care about. I can knock you into shape in a year if you're willing."

"But—but, I thought. . . ." I had got myself all muddled up, but I had to say it. "I thought you wanted a Holmes to ride Queenie in the Royal. I—I didn't think you'd be interested in anyone else."

I saw the pain cross his eyes like a shadow, and I wished I didn't have to keep putting my foot in it.

"No, you're not a Holmes," he said in a low voice. "But unfortunately, there are none of us left now to carry on the family tradition. Still life has to go on, and there's Queenie without a rider. She's a fine horse, one of the best I've owned. I don't want to sell her but, if I show her, she has to have a rider. It's either you or somebody else."

Feeling very humble I said, "I'll try not to let you down."

A ghost of a smile flickered over his stern face. He held out his hand and said, "Good enough. Let's shake on that."

My hand seemed very small in his, but I gripped it hard. Suddenly I found myself admiring this lonely, fierce man who had lost so much and refused to buckle under. Although I could never take the place of John, I vowed there and then that I would try and make him proud of me to soften his hurt a little. There was no other way to show him my gratitude.

With the bargain sealed, Mr. Holmes became business-like again. "I'll drop over at your house some time this evening," he told me briskly. "You can get back to work now."

I wanted to thank him again, but he was already walking

away with Jim leading Queenie, deep in discussion that probably had nothing to do with me at all.

I went back to my barn chores in a state of euphoria. It was a bit of an anticlimax, shoveling out muck, when I wanted to go berserk and run up and down the road calling out the good news to everyone who passed; but it was good for me. There was nothing like good honest toil to get my head out of the clouds, and my feet solidly planted on the earth again—and some little inward voice warned me that I ought to have all my wits firmly about me when I faced my father with the news.

¶ Hear from John

· 14 ·

My father thought I had made the whole thing up so that I wouldn't have to leave Grandma's. He burst out laughing when I told him.

I was indignant. "It's true!" I yelled up at him. He was sitting astride the roof of his tool shed nailing on shingles. "I didn't make it up. Mr. Holmes is coming over to see you later."

That shook him. He peered down at me suspiciously. "Oh, come on now, Joanna," he said shortly. "I wasn't born yesterday. If this is some sort of a hoax you've rigged up with your horsey friends, I can tell you it's not going to work. Why don't you resign yourself to the fact that you're leaving next week, and let that be an end to it?"

As calmly as possible I said, "Daddy, Mr. Holmes is not my horsey friend. When you meet him you'll see he isn't the kind of person to play jokes. He's serious. Now that John's gone, he wants somebody to ride Queenie, and he thinks I'm good enough."

"Nonsense!" My father hit a nail for emphasis, missed it and whacked his thumb. When he had finished swearing, he glared down at me. "If he wants you to stay he must have some ulterior motive. Probably wants to get a stable girl cheap. You're very young and green, Joanna. You mustn't believe everything everybody says to you."

I was through with being calm. Clenching my fists, I yelled up at him. "That's not true! I'm a good rider! I know I am!"

Maxwell and Julian sauntered up, attracted by the noise. Other people's arguments were a constant source of interest to them. They liked to compare them with their own.

"I expect he wants you for the white slave market," Maxwell predicted solemnly. "I don't suppose he's a stockbroker at all. I expect his farm is a front for a drug racket."

"What utter rubbish, Maxwell!" Father said irritably. "Who's been filling your head with such stuff?"

"You have, Dad," said Maxwell, innocently. "I read that article you wrote about crime and violence for the weekend magazine. You said that . . ."

"Never mind what I said!" exploded Father. "That article was not for the eyes of eight-year-olds!"

"Yes, but Dad, remember you said that comics were softening up our brains and we'd end up idiots if we didn't read something worthwhile now and then, so I thought . . ."

"I am not interested in what you thought!" Father threw the hammer onto the ground and followed it down the ladder. "I come down here for peace and quiet after slaving all week to keep you all in the luxuries to which you have accustomed yourselves, and I refuse to let you give me an ulcer. As far as I'm concerned, you're an ungrateful, delinquent lot. I'm going inside to get a beer, and kindly do not follow me!"

We watched him bleakly as he disappeared into the house. "Now he's good and mad," remarked Julian with a sigh. "What did you have to make up a stupid story like that for, Jo?"

I was going to protest, but then I thought it wasn't worth it. Instead I wandered off to the old barn, found a corner that hadn't yet been demolished and indulged in a bout of self-pity. Why could nothing be straightforward for me, like for other girls in other families? My only hope was to broach Mother when she came home from shopping.

By now she was almost immune to sudden shocks, but it was a bad time to tell her. There were hundreds of sandwiches to be cut for the party, and she was slightly distraught as usual.

"We'll worry about it later, dear," she told me, slapping butter recklessly on slices of bread. "Put the cookies on the plates, will you, and see if there's any corn left in the garden?"

It was no use appealing to Grandma or Margaret, either; they were just as busy, and obviously my future was of no interest to anyone. I did what I was told, but inside I was seething. If my father disgraced me by making a scene in front of Mr. Holmes, I decided I would follow John's example and run away from home.

Although I had been looking forward to it, I couldn't get into the spirit of the party. As the evening progressed, I went through agonies fearing that Mr. Holmes had changed his mind and wouldn't come, yet dreading what would happen if he did. The party seemed to be getting wilder by the minute, with music blaring out everywhere. Father was holding court in the kitchen. The young people really liked him for some reason, though he wasn't very popular with me at the moment. Mother seemed to be having a good time, too. The last I saw of her she was being serenaded by a lanky art student with a guitar, who called her "earth mother." Grandma and Mr. Archer were playing cribbage upstairs, probably wearing earplugs.

When the doorbell finally rang my courage deserted me. I fled into the basement and hid in the fruit cellar. I just couldn't face seeing Mr. Holmes's expression when he was precipitated without warning into this madhouse. Even worse than that, I dreaded what would happen when he confronted Father. They were both such strong-minded individuals, I had visions of fistfights and other dreadful things.

Suffering torments, I crouched in the cellar, waiting for the riot to begin overhead, but the music continued to seep through the ceiling, accompanied by muffled thumps and shouts of laughter. I was cold and miserable. At last, feeling ashamed of myself, I crept up the basement stairs and stuck my head around the door. For some obscure reason, Margaret and Wallace were sitting cross-legged in the passageway, balancing paper cups of water on their heads.

"Hey, Margaret!" I hissed in a staccato whisper. "What happened to Mr. Holmes?"

She jumped and the paper cup fell sideways, drenching Wallace. She glared at me. "I wish you would carry a bell or something, always creeping around!" Mopping up Wallace with a Kleenex, she said, "He's gone outside with Dad. Mother gave him a sandwich and a beer, and they've gone to look at the new barn."

"Oh," I said limply. I had worked myself up into such a

state, it was a bit of a letdown to know that my future hadn't been worth fighting over. Feeling rather silly, I elbowed my way through the melee in the kitchen and went outside.

Father was showing his tool shed to Mr. Holmes when I caught up with them. They were comparing techniques of relaxation. Father said he didn't think you could beat carpentry, while Mr. Holmes preferred raising horses, after which Father volunteered to show him Horse. Unseen and unnoticed, I trailed along after them to the new barn where Horse was already installed, with a blue ribbon tying up her bangs to celebrate the auspicious occasion. Mr. Holmes ran a practiced eye over her, looked at her teeth, and said tactfully that she wasn't a bad specimen as far as Quarter horses went, but slightly overweight. I couldn't stand the suspense any longer, so I cleared my throat loudly.

Father stared at me absentmindedly. "Oh, is that you, Joanna?" Catching on from my frantic signals behind Mr. Holmes's back, he said, "Oh, yes, we were supposed to be discussing you, weren't we?"

"Perhaps you'd like to come over to my place for a drink," suggested Mr. Holmes. "My father dabbles a bit in woodwork when he can find the time. He'd like to meet you."

"Very kind of you," murmured Father, and off they went again, without a word about me. I was beginning to have all kinds of doubts about my self-importance. I went into the barn and buried my face in Horse's warm neck, not knowing whether to laugh or cry, or to quietly have hysterics all on my own.

But it was all settled as easily as that. Against all probabilities, Father and Mr. Holmes took to each other right away. Mother said they were so completely opposite in temperament, they complemented each other but, whatever the reason, they seemed to do each other good. Mr. Holmes loosened up in Father's company, and Father no longer scoffed about country bumpkins and bucolic tastes once he had seen the inside of the house at Holmwood Farms. Mr. Holmes convinced Father that I had the makings of a promising rider, and at last I came in for some share of the attention, although Father swore I got my talent from him, since he had been on a pony once when he was five and distinctly remembered not falling off.

But all that mattered to me was that I was allowed to stay with Grandma. I missed everybody very much at first, but Mr. Archer and Grandma made a great fuss over me, and I didn't have time to be lonely once school started. Jim gave me a lesson every day after school, and Mr. Holmes took over at weekends. He was stricter than Jim, and quite relentless. The first time he had me out, he pulled me apart so much that I almost broke down in tears, convinced I was hopeless, but I stuck it out and I think I earned his respect. I guessed he was testing me, making sure I was worth his effort before he wasted any more time on me.

After a while a strange sort of friendship developed between us. I always had to groom Queenie after my lessons, however grueling they had been. At first Mr. Holmes used to watch me like a hawk to see I wasn't skipping any of the harder tasks, like picking out her hooves, but gradually he relaxed and began to talk to me.

Mostly we talked about John. There had been no news of him, and he might have vanished off the face of the earth. Now that he was gone, Mr. Holmes seemed hungry to learn more about him, and I couldn't help thinking how sad it was that he had waited until it was too late to get to know his son.

Once, just as I was leaving, he said impulsively, "Joanna, I wish I had gotten to know you better while John was here";

then, obviously embarrassed, he limped quickly away, but I was filled with a warm glow of affection for him. I wished I had had the courage to run after him and give him a hug, because he was such a proud and lonely man and needed someone to love and understand him.

It wasn't too long before my family starting turning up every weekend. Father wouldn't admit that the city's charms were wearing thin, but it looked like that to me. The Holmeses invited us to dinner, and then we had to exchange invitations, and soon we were shuffling back and forth like old friends. The beautiful house that had once awed me speechless was now almost as familiar to me as my own. I began to look forward to the weekend visits, even though it meant getting out camp cots and disarranging the household regularly every Friday night. However, Grandma and Mr. Archer didn't seem to mind, or if they did they were too polite to say so.

I was so happy and busy I hardly noticed the days speeding by until one day I noticed the leaves were all gone, and the next day it snowed. There was a covered arena at Holmwood Farms, so the weather made no difference to me. I had my daily lesson just the same. My family was coming down for the Christmas holidays, and Grandma had asked the Holmeses to dinner on Christmas Eve. Wallace was asked, too, for Margaret's sake, although he had to be back in time to spend Christmas Day with his own family. I was really kept hopping, what with helping Grandma bake and shop, and my riding and schoolwork. Then we had to decorate the house and trim the tree. Mr. Archer, who was walking quite well with the aid of a stick, helped me tie up fir boughs with red ribbon and shiny bells, and we hung them up all over the house and on the front door. It looked like we were going to have a real old-fashioned Christmas.

Coming home from my lesson on Christmas Eve, I ran all the way over the hard, crisp snow because there were so many final preparations to help Grandma with before my family arrived and bedlam was let loose. I was pulling off my snowy boots in the kitchen when the phone rang. "I'll get it!" I called out to Grandma, who was upstairs. I was in such a good mood I called out "Merry Christmas!" into the receiver before I even asked who was calling.

There was a long pause at the other end; then a voice said uncertainly, "Joanna, is that you?"

A funny, tingling sensation ran up my spine. "Who's that?" I asked breathlessly.

"It's John."

I stared at the phone as though it were playing tricks on me. All I could do was repeat stupidly, "John?"

"Yes, John. John Holmes, remember? I used to live next door to you."

I could picture him shaking his head in mock exasperation, the way he had always done when I was being especially dim-witted, and suddenly there was no more doubt in my mind.

"John!" I cried excitedly. "It's good to hear from you! Merry Christmas!"

"Same to you," he said. "I had a feeling you might be spending Christmas at your grandmother's. How's all the family?"

"Fine, just fine!" I knew there were a million things I ought to say to him, but the sudden shock of hearing his voice had wiped everything out of my mind.

"Say hello to them for me, won't you? I can't talk long because I'm working and we're pretty busy. Have you—have you heard how my folks are?"

He was talking so quickly I couldn't collect my

thoughts. I had a horrible feeling he was going to ring off at any moment. "Where are you?" I cried, suddenly coming to my senses. "What are you doing?"

"Look, Jo," he said in an urgent voice, "I've got to run. We're up to our ears here. I'm working in a restaurant, and it's full up with Christmas shoppers." He must have heard my gasp, because he said hastily, "You don't have to tell my dad that. It's only temporary anyway, to get a bit of money behind me to pay for my studies. I've sold my car, but that won't last forever. I'm doing all right, Jo. Just tell them that if you see them, okay?"

I was desperate to keep him on the line. "John," I pleaded with him, "why don't you come home and talk to your father?" I had been going to tell him how Mr. Holmes had changed, but John cut me off sharply, not giving me a chance.

"I've made the break, Jo, finally, and I'm going through with it. When I've made it on my own, I'll go back and see them, but not before, and you can tell them that, too, if you like."

I knew from the steely tone of his voice that if I persisted in talking about his father he would probably hang up on me; yet somehow I knew I had to get them together so that John could see the change for himself. The wheels of my mind started turning frantically. "Well listen, John," I gabbled on, "why don't you come and see us, come tonight after work? Are you far from here?"

I heard the hesitation in his voice. "N-no. I could probably hitch there with luck in a couple of hours."

"Well, come then," I begged him. "We'd all love to see you, and it'd be dark so you wouldn't have to worry. Wallace is coming, and he has to go home tonight, so he could give you a lift back."

There was another pause, and I could hear the background noises of a crowded restaurant, dishes rattling and the hum of many voices. I just couldn't imagine John waiting on people or washing dishes. He had seemed so proud when I first met him, so far above me in every way. Now he said, almost wistfully, "You're tempting me, Jo. I'm not going to have a very wild Christmas here by myself, and I'm working tomorrow. Can I trust your family?"

"Of course you can. You know you can," I said, and I was right. It was me he couldn't trust, and I felt lower than a worm when I heard the undisguised relief in his voice that he wasn't going to have to spend Christmas all alone. "Okay, then, I'll try and make it. It'll be great to see your family again. I missed you."

Somebody called him then, and he had to hang up. "I missed you, too," I said miserably, as I put the receiver down. I was getting to be as scheming as Maxwell and Julian without their stamina for it. My stomach already felt queasy when I thought what I had done. I hadn't actually lied to John, only neglected to tell him his grandfather and father were coming to supper as well; but what if there was a terrible scene? What if I ruined Christmas for everybody and made John despise me for the rest of his life? Now that I had a few minutes to think about the consequences of my rash action, I wanted to cut out my tongue, but it was too late for that now. I couldn't reach John and tell him not to come because he hadn't told me where he was, and I couldn't bring myself to confess to my family what I had done, in case they would be furious with me. All I could hope and pray for was that he wouldn't get a ride. The more I thought about it, much as I longed to see John again, that seemed the only solution for saving everybody's Christmas.

Homecoming

· 15 ·

By evening I had worked myself up into such a state, I felt I
would snap in two if anyone touched me. My family,
rambunctious as usual, had descended on us and, in the
ensuing noise and confusion, heightened by the festive
season, no one seemed to notice that my gaiety was more
than a bit forced. Once or twice I was on the verge of
seeking out Mother and spilling the secret that was weighing
me down so, but I could never get her alone. Father, of
course, was out of the question. I could just imagine him
flying through the roof and not coming down until New
Year's.

The Holmeses arrived full of good cheer, bringing with
them a marvelous hamper of fruit tied up with red cellophane
and ribbon. The sight of John's father, so smiling and
agreeable, didn't help my nervous state. It seemed to me that

he had finally come to accept John's absence and was beginning to make a new life for himself as Jim had said he must do. And here was I going to stir everything up again and cause heavens knows what trouble!

Grandma had cooked a wonderful meal, but it might have been sawdust and putty as far as I was concerned but, when the second course was over and John still hadn't come, I began to perk up a little. Surely he would have been here by now if he had been able to get a ride. John's father stood up and proposed a toast. Smiling at me he said, "To a wonderful young lady with a great future ahead of her!"

I was feeling so wrought up and guilty by then that the tears welled up and everyone teased me for being so emotional. Then Grandma brought in the Christmas cake and, while she was cutting it, the doorbell rang!

I wanted to get up and run to the door and tell John to go away, but my knees had turned to jelly. I felt myself turning cold, and I had a horrible feeling I was going to faint. I hardly knew who went to answer the door, but I think it was Margaret, because she was standing there saying excitedly, "Look everybody! Look who's here!"

John was standing beside her, taking in the scene before him. I couldn't take my eyes from his face. One minute he was smiling; then the smile died slowly and, for one brief moment, our eyes met. His look accused me more than any words could have done. Before anyone had gotten over the shock of seeing him, he had turned around and walked out again. The room started reeling around me. I heard, rather than saw, Mr. Holmes gasp, scrape back his chair and limp out with long strides after John. The next thing I knew I was lying on the floor, and everyone was fussing around me. Father picked me up and carried me upstairs. He laid me on the bed, and I burst into uncontrollable sobs. Mother tried to calm me, but it was some time before I could confess what I had done.

"But that wasn't so terrible, dear," said Mother, surprised. "You should have told us and Mr. Holmes so we would have been prepared, but it's nothing to get so upset about."

"But John will hate me now!" I wailed. "And I've spoiled Christmas for everybody!"

"Nonsense!" said Father. "You're dramatizing everything as usual, Joanna, and all you've succeeded in doing is making yourself ill and worrying everybody. Mr. Holmes and his son are both civilized people."

"Then why did John go away like that!" I exclaimed tragically.

"Well, I suppose he had a guilty conscience and didn't know how to cope with it on the spur of the moment. Anyway, he's talking to his father now. Everything is quite under control."

Margaret opened the door and peeped in to see how I was.

"There's nothing wrong with her that a little common sense wouldn't have prevented in the first place," Father told her. "How are things down below?"

"Mr. Holmes just came back in. He said John would like to see Joanna if she's okay."

I sat up aghast. "I can't! I don't want to see him! I look terrible! I look a mess!"

"No you don't, dear, you look woebegone and interesting," Mother reassured me. She took out her compact and powdered my scarlet nose. "There! I really think you should see him."

I felt too weak to argue. They steered me downstairs on

wobbly legs. Grandma and Mr. Archer patted my back and made soothing noises, and Wallace offered to give me yoga lessons so that I would learn to keep my cool under all circumstances. Julian and Maxwell just stared at me with clinical interest, hoping no doubt that I was going to entertain them by keeling over again. Mr. Holmes was in the front room talking to his father, but John had stayed outside. Everybody helped me with my coat and boots, and then, heartlessly, they shoved me through the door.

The night was crisp, the snowy fields illuminated by moonlight. John was leaning on the fence looking over at Holmwood Farms. My footsteps were so silent on the snow, he didn't hear me come up until I was right behind him.

"Hi, John," I said. My voice came out in a kind of a croak.

He turned and looked at me. "That was a sneaky trick you played on me, Joanna," he said coldly.

I lowered my head in shame. "I know, but I wanted you to come home, and I couldn't think of any other way to get you here. Your dad's changed, John. You've been talking to him. You must see that."

He looked at me a moment longer, then turned back to the fence. I wondered what he had wanted to see me for, if he wasn't going to talk to me. Desperately I said, "You're not mad, are you, because I've taken your place?"

"No, I'm not mad. I'm glad you and my father get along so well together. It eases my conscience."

There was another awkward silence; then John suddenly whirled around and said impatiently, "Look, Jo, I finally made the break! On my own, with no help from anyone, I managed to get myself accepted into veterinary college. I'm free now. No strings attached at all. You don't know how good that feels."

"Oh, John, that's great!" I was really happy for him, but that wasn't enough. "Couldn't you come home, though?" I begged him. "Your father really missed you! He really did!"

"Oh, sure, he wants me to come home," said John. "He's changed all right. He's even offered to pay my way through college. But what about that damn Holmes pride of his? How do I know it isn't just a trick to lure me back again into the same old rut? I don't suppose I'd have the guts to do it again, and he knows it."

He was making me angry. "You've forgotten," I said. "There's me now."

"Don't count on it, Jo. You're not a Holmes, however well you ride. If I come back, how do you know he won't drop you like a hot brick?"

I really saw red then. "You talk about the Holmes pride," I flung at him, "and you're full of it! You'd rather slog in some greasy little restaurant and take ten times as long to get through college, just so you can boast that you did it on your own, no matter who you hurt! Your father was big enough to realize when he was wrong, but you're not! I'm sorry for him, having a son like you. I don't want to talk to you anymore. You've ruined my Christmas. Why don't you go back to your poky little garret, or wherever you're living, and leave us alone, because we were having a darned good time without you!"

I turned and ran stumbling through the knee-deep snow. It was difficult, and I couldn't see where I was going because of my tears. I slipped and fell face first into the icy snow. John came after and helped me up. He brushed me off and wiped away my tears, which kept coming back.

"You know," he said, "you're the worst crybaby I've ever met."

"Well, it's not my fault," I blubbered. "All I want is for

everybody to be happy, but people just don't seem to want to be."

John laughed. "You're a real little Pollyanna, aren't you?" He brushed some snow off the tip of my nose and said, "Okay, I won't tease you anymore. I've already told my father I'll come back and we'll try again. Of course I'll be away at college, but weekends I'll be up here."

"Oh, John!" I cried, and then I was angry. "Why didn't you tell me? Why did you make me believe . . . ?"

He stopped me with a hand over my mouth. "Because you deserved it," he said, and then, more seriously, "and, anyway, I guess I still am a bit afraid, Joanna. I'm sure there has to be a catch somewhere. You know what my father was like. Can people really change that quickly?"

"It wasn't quickly," I reminded him. "It was days and weeks and months. It was hard for him, John, I know it was, but he's changed all right. And so have you, and he knows it. He wouldn't risk losing you again."

He studied my earnest face in the moonlight, and slowly smiled. "You're right, Jo. I shouldn't go back with reservations. It has to be a clean start or it isn't fair. I missed him, too, you know, and my grandfather. I think that now we've got this riding thing straightened out, we can be friends. I hope so anyway." He gave me a whimsical grin. "I don't think I was really cut out for working in restaurants, but it was good for me. I never really appreciated what I had before."

"I did," I told him. "You don't know how much I envied you."

"And now you don't have to anymore." John put his arm around me and I felt safe and warm and happy, as though I belonged there. "Shall we go back to the party, Jo? I imagine they're waiting for us. Do you feel all right, now?"

"I feel wonderful," I said. "I never felt better in my whole life."

So we had a good time that Christmas Eve after all, the sort of time you remember always, and next day we met again and went tobogganing on the snowy hills of Holmwood Farms. Father came with us and enjoyed himself more than anybody. John came back with us for lunch and, while we were all warming our frozen feet by the fire and drinking steaming mugs of soup, Father said, "There's something to be said for the simple joys of country life. You know, I feel ten years younger."

I couldn't resist saying wickedly, "Don't you miss your sauna, Daddy, and your heated swimming pool?"

I think it was the first time I had ever seen him look sheepish. "All right," he said, blustering to hide his embarrassment, "so I'll admit there might be something to living in the country after all, but unfortunately one needs a substantial down payment to buy a decent house with a bit of land attached to it and, with four voracious youngsters making demands on me, I don't see how I will ever acquire it—unless I send you all out to work."

I stared at him in disbelief. "You mean you'd really *like* to, Daddy?" I couldn't believe this was my father talking. "But if you owned a house, you couldn't be traveling all the time, then what would you write about?"

Grandma, who had caught the tail end of the conversation, said with a little snort of disapproval, "There's plenty of things happening around here. I've never seen the necessity of scurrying off to the other end of the earth to get material to write about. That's just a waste of good money, in my opinion."

The Christmas spirit must have gotten into Father because, instead of getting into one of his endless arguments with Grandma, he just said firmly, "Well, since the question of buying a house in the country and settling down is way beyond my means, I don't see the point of carrying on this conversation any longer."

John caught my eye and winked. He was used to my family now. "Why don't we go for an old-fashioned sleigh ride?" he said, deftly changing the subject. "We have a sleigh in the old barn. It hasn't been used for years, but it should be all right."

We all thought that was a marvelous idea. "Could Horse take us?" suggested Maxwell eagerly. "She needs the exercise. She's getting as fat as a pig."

John said it was fine with him, so off we went to the barn to fetch her. Grandma had to prepare Christmas dinner, and Mr. Archer stayed behind to keep her company, but everybody else bundled up ready for the fun. John hadn't seen Horse since September. When we led her proudly out of her stall in the new barn, he looked at her, and then looked again. I thought his eyes were going to pop out of his head. Then slowly his shoulders began to shake, and he stood silently convulsed in laughter. We were all very hurt. We knew Horse was a bit overweight, but we didn't think she looked that funny.

"You'd be fat, too," I told him huffily, "if you didn't do anything all day except eat. The boys aren't here to exercise her anymore, and I don't have the time."

"I don't think exercise will fix what ails her, Jo," said John, and off he went again into another fit of merriment.

"What do you mean?" I retorted indignantly. I thought he was being extremely rude, not at all the gentleman that Grandma professed him to be.

"Well," he said slowly, squinting his eyes at me, "do you remember one day last May, when I came across a certain young lady who shall be nameless, bawling her head off because she couldn't catch her horse?"

"Yes," I said stupidly, "but . . ."

"And do you remember why she couldn't catch her horse? Because a certain stallion, our prize stud in fact, had jumped the fence and was giving her a merry dance. Well, Jo, I think you're going to have a legacy of that day, the pitter-patter of little hooves around the barn."

My hand flew to my open mouth in horror. "Oh, my goodness! Oh, no!" I looked at him aghast. "What will your grandfather say? Won't we have to pay a stud fee? Oh, that's terribly expensive, isn't it?"

John was trying very hard to keep a straight face. "I don't know what the procedure is in a case like this," he said. "It has never happened before. I'll have to ask my grandfather."

Maxwell and Julian were staring at us wide eyed. "You mean," squealed Maxwell, "that Horse is going to have a *baby?*"

"It looks very much like it to me," said John.

"Whoopee!" cried Maxwell. He looked at Julian, and they began to leap around clapping their hands and shrieking, "Horse is going to have a baby! Horse is going to have a foal!"

"Now *just* a minute!" said Father, putting his foot down. "Before you go off the deep end, I hope you don't think you can keep it!"

"Oh, but Dad, you could pay the stud fee, couldn't you?" pleaded Maxwell. "Couldn't you, Dad?"

Father groaned and struck his forehead helplessly. "Stud fees! That's all I need. You'll have me in the poorhouse yet, between the lot of you. And where, might I ask, were you thinking of keeping this new arrival? Not in the city, I trust?"

"Now there's no need to be sarcastic, dear," said Mother. She had gone all soft and protective toward Horse. "Shouldn't she have special food or something? I wonder how she's feeling. Obviously we can't take her out with the sleigh now."

"Of course we can," said John briskly. "She's not sick, and she won't be having the foal until April. Exercise will be good for her."

He took charge of Horse and led her down the road to Holmwood Farms. Mother protested all the way, but the rest of us were strangely subdued, awed by the miracle of new life that had happened to our silly old Horse. We were very gentle with her as we helped harness her into the old sleigh. Once it had been bright red, but the paint was fading now, and there were tears in the upholstery. However, the harness bells still jingled merrily, and the runners slid easily over the hard-packed snow. After being cooped up for so long in the barn, Horse acted like a two-year-old. We sped up and down the hilly fields, with the cold freezing our noses and the warm rugs hugging us tight. The only jarring note was Mother, who kept begging John to take it slower for Horse's sake. At last Father said in disgust, "Would you like us to get out and pull the sleigh, dear, while Horse rides?"

Mother said coyly, "Now you're being silly, dear. You men just don't understand things like this. One of the best things about having babies is being pampered. I should know."

She had Father there. He subsided into his blanket, muttering vague threats about dropping her off so that she could start knitting bootees. Horse was the only one who seemed quite unperturbed. I had never seen her with so much energy. Motherhood was agreeing with her already.

Back in the barn, we fed her and brushed her tenderly,

then went into the house to break the great news to Grandma and Mr. Archer. They greeted us in the doorway of the sun porch. Something about the way they looked, half-coy, half-smug, made Mother say suspiciously, as though they were a couple of teenagers, "What have you two been up to?"

Grandma looked mightily pleased with herself. Fixing her eyes on Father, she said triumphantly, "I'm calling your bluff, Herbert. You say you'd be willing to settle down in the country if you could afford a house. Well, I'll rent you this one for half the price you're paying for that fancy apartment of yours. Now what have you got to say to that?"

Startled, Father couldn't say anything for a moment. He huffed and spluttered and finally blurted out, "Well—well that's decent of you, Mother, but it wouldn't work out, you know. Eight people living in one house is just too many. I mean, it's all right for weekends, but . . . ."

"But there wouldn't be eight people," Grandma cut in smugly. "Because I shall be leaving in May."

"Leaving!" We stared at her in dismay. "Grandma, where are you going?"

Mr. Archer chuckled. He stepped forward and put his arm around Grandma, and she actually blushed. "Not very far, my dears. Just across the fields. You see, this good lady is worried I'm not capable of looking after myself without getting into more trouble so, to put her mind at rest, I've asked her to come and look after me when my house becomes vacant again."

"You mean . . . ?" gasped Mother, but she didn't have to finish because Mr. Archer, with an affectionate smile for Grandma, said, "Yes, I have asked her to be my wife, and she has made me a very proud and happy man by accepting."

A Horse of Our Own

· 16 ·

Poor Father didn't really stand a chance, not with all of us banding against him and squashing his objections one by one; but I think if he had been really against the idea, we might not have overruled him so easily. We never had before. The fact was he rather fancied himself as a country gentleman and, once he had made his token fuss, he started planning extensive improvements to Grandma's house. I wondered when he was going to find the time to write.

Grandma and Mr. Archer planned to get married on the first of May, when the lease on their house was up, and Father had the place in the city until then, so everything worked out beautifully. John came home every weekend, and the Holmeses were a happy family again. If I had been one of them, they couldn't have taken more interest in my riding progress. Their hopes for me were so great, sometimes I was afraid I would never be able to live up to them.

Mr. Holmes was counting on me being eligible for the Royal that year. The horse show season started in May, and the shows were classed according to importance. To be eligible for the Royal, a horse had to win a red ribbon in one Class A, two Class B or three Class C shows. In equitation, or skill of horsemanship, the rider was judged separately from the horse and accumulated points over the season. I knew Queenie was good, the best, but sometimes I wondered if I was worthy of her.

"Now you listen, sweetheart," Jim said to me, after I had confessed my feelings of inadequacy to him for the hundredth time. "A horse and rider complement each other, so if Queenie's doing well, give yourself some credit. Mr. Holmes wouldn't be wasting his time on you if he didn't think you were worth it. He doesn't believe in frittering his time away just for the fun of it."

I knew it, but that almost made things worse. The fact was I was becoming increasingly nervous as the year progressed. John came to see me ride one Saturday and afterward, when I was brushing Queenie down, he said to me, "You really looked good out there, Jo. I think my dad's picked himself a winner."

Coming at a time when I was so unsure of myself, his words acted like a tonic to me. Impulsively, I leaned over the stall and gave him a dusty kiss. He laughed and blew a wisp of hair out of my eyes.

"When you're up there at the top, I hope you won't forget us humble people who gave you your start."

"Humble, my foot!" I said, but it made me very happy to hear him say that. A year ago I would have died of happiness, but I had things to stay alive for now.

February passed into March, with alternate thaws that exposed the green spears of crocuses peeping through the mud, and then blizzards plunging us into the depths of winter again. Horse grew rounder and rounder until we felt she was in danger of rolling over sideways. At the end of March we moved her over to Holmwood Farms where she would have the best of care.

When we had told old Mr. Holmes about the foal, he had had a good laugh about it. He had assured Father that there would be no stud fee, since it had been an accident, but, feeling rather guilty as we did, we had not liked to press the question of ownership. Because the unborn foal had been sired by a prize stallion, we felt that Holmwood Farms should have first claim to it and, much to Julian and Maxwell's disgust, Father forbade them to bring up the matter.

"Mr. Holmes has been very decent about the whole thing," he told them sternly. "Joanna had no right to leave Horse on their property, and I won't have you taking advantage of his kindness by putting him in the embarrassing position of having to refuse you. That foal might be worth a lot of money and, if Mr. Holmes wants to keep it or sell it at some later date, he has a perfect right to do so."

Father was right, of course. The Holmes family had been so good to us in every way, it would be awful if they thought we were greedy or grasping. Still, it was a little hard to take. Horse would be going with Mr. Archer and Grandma when they left, and our beautiful new barn, built with our own sweat and toil, would be empty, just crying out for a horse of its own.

Still, there was too much happening to fret about things like that. My first show was coming up in May, and there was Grandma's wedding. She had chosen a beautiful day, one meant for celebration. The sun shone warm, holding a promise of summer. The daffodils were a riot of bloom down the front path, and buds on the trees were swelling into leaves. We had filled the house and the little country church with spring flowers. Margaret and I were attending Grandma, and we wore dresses of yellow chiffon with posies of violets. Even Wallace turned up in a suit for once. It was a sort of muddy purple, which clashed horribly with our dresses, but we could appreciate the compliment he was paying us.

"Feast your eyes, folks," he said, "because this is the one and only time you'll ever see me in a suit, so help me!"

"What about at your own wedding, Wallace?" hinted Margaret coyly.

Wallace, in his collar and tie, seemed about to strangle, and I felt rather sorry for Margaret, but I don't think she really minded. I think that next to writing first chapters, her second-best hobby was reforming people, and she had done such a good job on Wallace already, there was probably hope for her yet.

And so, with a robin singing its heart out on the hawthorn tree beside the church door, Grandma became Mrs. Archer. It was a simple ceremony. Besides us, the Holmes family was there and a few of Grandma's friends. The church smelled of wax polish, flowers and candles. Mother cried, and Julian and Maxwell were disgusted, but for once it looked as if something we had undertaken was going to go off without a hitch.

But, of course, that was too much to hope for. Halfway through the service, I became aware of a quiet commotion taking place at the rear of the church. Turning surreptitiously, I saw one of the ushers trying to close the door on Jim, who was trying equally hard to catch my attention. I just managed to catch the words, "Hurry—Horse!" before he was edged out, but Maxwell and Julian had heard, too. Before long the news was being passed from pew to pew that Horse was in foal.

An undercurrent of excitement swept around the church and communicated itself to Grandma and Mr. Archer, who, much to the surprise of the minister, began to gabble their responses at a great rate. While we were almost tripping over ourselves to get into the vestry to sign the register, Grandma whispered to the startled minister, "We've got to hurry! The baby's due!" and sent the poor man into shock. The beautiful wedding disintegrated into a shambles. We couldn't actually run down the aisle because that would have been unseemly but, once outside, the proprieties were forgotten. We raced to our respective cars, Grandma and Mr. Archer included, yelling to the drivers, "Hurry! Hurry!" and tore down the quiet country road more like a drag race than a wedding party. At Holmwood Farms we squealed into the driveway and disgorged ourselves, squelching through the mud with no thought for our silver wedding slippers. Mine came off somewhere, and I ended up crossing the paddock in great bounds in my stocking feet.

Jim and the local vet met us at the big barn, their faces wreathed in smiles. "All over," said Jim proudly. "A beautiful little colt. No trouble at all."

Reverently we tiptoed down the barn to Horse's stall, and there it was, the funniest little thing imaginable, all knobby legs and big brown eyes, teetering around on perfect miniature hooves, while Horse leaned contentedly against the wall, chewing hay. While we looked on with adoration, John's father went in to inspect the foal. He announced that Horse had produced a little champion.

"Quite obviously she intended it as a wedding present for you, Mrs. Archer," chuckled old Mr. Holmes. "I'd say that was perfect timing, wouldn't you?"

Grandma looked at him in amazement. Her flowery bonnet was all askew and her brocade dress was sadly splattered with mud, but her cheeks were as rosy as a young bride's.

"Why, Mr. Holmes, you don't mean that, do you?" she said.

"Of course I do dear lady," he said gallantly. "But don't thank me. Thank Horse. I had nothing to do with it."

Grandma gave him a radiant smile. "Well," she said, "in that case I must consult my husband." She drew Mr. Archer aside and, when they came back, they were grinning like two Cheshire cats. "We have decided," Grandma announced, "that two old people like us will have enough to do looking after one horse so, as soon as he is old enough to leave his mother, we would like to present this little fellow to our grandchildren, in memory of our marriage and all they did to help bring it about."

We all rushed at her, whooping, and smothered her. Her wedding hat lost its last mooring and lay trampled on the floor, but nobody noticed. I stole a look at Father. He looked puffed up with pride as he gazed over the stall at our very own horse. He couldn't have been prouder if he had been the father.

"Welcome to the horsey set, Daddy," I said wickedly.

He shot me a murderous look, but his heart wasn't in it. "By golly!" he thundered. "We'll have to think up a suitable name for this little fellow!"

"Horse the Second!" piped up Maxwell.

"No!" I wailed. "No!"

But I was outnumbered, and it didn't really matter. I had learned by now that a name wasn't important. When a horse could come into somebody's life and change it completely within the space of a year, making every little wish come true, then it was a pretty special horse, whatever its name was.

After the others had gone into the wedding breakfast, I was the last to leave the barn. I leaned over the stall and stroked the velvety nose of the foal. It wasn't at all nervous. It nuzzled me and tried to lean against my hand. It was another Horse all right. I felt so warm and happy inside, I laughed to myself.

"Hi, Horse the Second," I said. "Welcome to our family!"

Almost a year to the day after I had first seen John and Queenie ride over the hill, I entered my first horse show. It was a Class A show and Mr. Holmes had entered me in two events, the Junior Handy Working Hunter, where competitors were judged on performance and hunting soundness, and the Open Jump, where time was the deciding factor. We had moved into Grandma's house the week before, and everybody congregated there to wish me luck. Jim had already gone ahead with Queenie, and I was to ride with the Holmeses in their shiny white convertible while the rest of our family slummed it, dividing themselves up between our little English car and Wallace's lurid Volkswagen. I had a new outfit for the occasion, and everyone commented on how elegant I looked, although I was so nervous I was practically paralyzed. Only John, sitting in the back seat with me and holding my hand, kept me from panicking.

"Take it easy, Jo," he said. "Relax!"

"You're a fine one to talk," I mumbled.

"It was different for me," he said. "I was forced to do something against my will, but this is what you've always wanted, Jo. This is your big day."

"I've got holes in my head," I moaned. "I should have stuck to my crochet."

But once we were at the showgrounds it was better. This time I was not an outsider, but part of it. The enclosure where the horse trailers were parked was like a gypsy encampment. People were erecting shelters, brewing up on little stoves and visiting each other companionably. A constant procession of riders led their mounts through the bivouacs to the practice ring and back, and they smiled at me with friendly curiosity. Since John had backed out of the competition circuit there was much speculation about me, and for a while I enjoyed being the cause of so much interest. Then the public started arriving and the show opened with the Junior Pony trials, and I would gladly have traded my new Harris tweed jacket and tan breeches, my smart leather boots and hard hat for a one-way ticket to South America.

The Hunter classes began at three o'clock. I took Queenie out into the practice ring to warm up a bit, and then I had to report for my jumping order in the Handy Working Hunter trials. I was number seven, which John told me was lucky. I think he would have said that, whatever number I picked, because by then I was having a bad case of the dithers.

"I'll let your father down!" I wailed.

John squeezed my hand. "No you won't. You wouldn't dare. It's got to be a red ribbon and nothing less, remember? My father knew what he was doing when he took you on."

Far from cheering me up, I felt I was carrying a millstone around my neck. With good wishes ringing in my ears, I mounted Queenie but I had never felt so totally alone. I was carrying the good name of three generations of Holmeses on my shoulders, and the burden was too heavy for me. I took my place waiting for my call. The course didn't look too difficult to me, if only I could conquer my nerves. None of the jumps were over three foot six, and they were shaped like walls and hedges and ditches to resemble the hazards of the hunt. I had jumped far worse in my time.

"Number seven on deck!" echoed the loudspeaker, and I took my place in front of the gate. I was a quivering mass of nerves. The girl in front of me rode off the course and gave me a nod of encouragement, and then it was me out there with everyone's eyes on me. I headed Queenie for the first jump, trying to remember everything I had been taught, when suddenly she pranced sideways and reared. I had to rein hard to control her. We tried again but she balked, snorting and tossing her head. It was terrible. I fought her, but I couldn't do a thing with her. Dimly, over my frustration, I heard the whistle blow, which meant I had used up my starting time and had been eliminated. I was so mortified I didn't remember riding out of the ring. All I could think of was that it was all over before it had even begun. Joanna Longfellow, who had been going to blaze a trail of glory right up to the Royal and beyond, hadn't been able to take one jump!

All I wanted to do was run away and hide. I didn't know how I was going to face Mr. Holmes, after having made a laughingstock of his name. I saw them coming toward me, and I didn't know where to look. I bit my lip hard, but I couldn't stop the tears trickling down. "She wouldn't jump!" I sobbed. "She just wouldn't jump!"

Jim took Queenie's bridle. He was nervous, too, because, after all, he had been responsible for suggesting me to Mr. Holmes. "She wouldn't jump because you were holding her back," he said in exasperation. "What got into you, Joanna? You can do better than that, you know you can!"

"Go easy on her," John said sharply. "It's only her first time, for heaven's sake! She's got stage fright. She'll be all right in the Open Jump."

But I wasn't going to make a fool out of myself again. "No I won't!" I cried out. "I'm not going on again!" I jumped from the saddle and thrust the reins into Jim's hand. "I'm sorry. I can't! I'll just keep letting you down. I'm just not good enough!"

I turned to run, but Mr. Holmes put out a hand and stopped me. "Come on, Joanna," he said firmly. "You and I are going to have a little talk."

He led me away and we walked twice around the perimeter of the showgrounds, he holding my arm tightly in case I should try to escape, and me sniffing spasmodically like a five-year-old kid and wiping my nose on my beautiful new Harris tweed sleeve.

"What makes you think you'll be letting us down?" he asked curiously, after a while.

"Because I will!" I exclaimed, heartbroken. "I made a fool out of you back there! Everybody was expecting me to be so good because you ditched John for me, and I was terrible! I was just terrible!"

There was another silence while we walked a few more paces. Then Mr. Holmes said quietly, "I didn't ditch John, Joanna. He ditched me—and we both of us know why. Don't you think I learned anything from that experience?"

I looked at him stupidly. I wasn't feeling my best, at that moment. "You wanted me to win, didn't you?" I asked him.

"Joanna, it doesn't matter to me whether you win or not."

I stopped and stared at him. I was actually a little hurt. "Then why did you take all that trouble with me?" I exclaimed. "I thought it was important to you. All you could

174

talk about was getting me and Queenie in the Royal this year. After all, Queenie comes from Holmwood Farms, even if I don't, and you would get some of the credit for her. . . ."

I was babbling on again, hardly knowing what I was saying. Mr. Holmes took me by the shoulders and shook me gently. "Joanna, Joanna," he said sorrowfully, "you don't know what you're talking about. I nearly lost John, pressing him too much for my own fulfillment. Do you think I want to risk that with you? You may not realize this, but the day John met you, that was the best thing that ever happened to the Holmes family."

I was quite astounded. "But you took so much trouble with me!" I said wonderingly.

Mr. Holmes smiled. "Can't you allow me the privilege for once in my life of doing something unselfish, Joanna? I wanted to make you happy, that's all. You are in no way obligated to me to win, or to place, or even to ride in shows at all if you don't want to. If you've gained some pleasure and a sense of achievement in learning to ride well, that's reward enough for me."

As I stared at him I was conscious of a feeling of lightness. There was no millstone around my neck any longer. "It's been wonderful," I said humbly. "It's been the best year in my whole life."

"Thank you, Joanna. That's all I want to know." Mr. Holmes patted my cheek and smiled at me. "Well, what about it? Are you going in for the Open Jump, or do you want to go home now?"

"I don't want to go home," I said. "I want to try again."

"Good girl," he said. "That's what I thought you'd say."

So there I was at four o'clock, on deck again awaiting my turn, and feeling somehow that nothing could hold me back now. I was on my own, but I was not alone any longer. This was all for me, and yet in a way it was for Mr. Holmes, too, and John and his grandfather; for my family, too, and Mr. Archer and Wallace Pindlebury—all the wonderful people who had kept faith in me and restored my faith in myself.

The Open Jump was timed for speed and, as soon as the gate opened and I was in the ring, I was conscious of nothing but the challenge ahead of me that was just beginning. Queenie and I rode like the wind. The jumps were higher this time, but they seemed like nothing at all. We did all eight of them in record time with no faults and, when the applause sounded in my ears as I rode out, I felt so happy and fulfilled I could have turned around and jumped them all again as an encore.

So Queenie got her red ribbon in an A show, and Mr. Holmes told me that if I went on riding like that there was absolutely no doubt whatsoever that I would compete in the Royal that year.

There isn't much to say after that, because this story is only about the first year, and the first triumph is always the best no matter how wonderful the following ones are; but that evening John and I slipped out from the celebration party that was being held for me at Holmwood Farms. We crossed the field where I had first met him, and climbed the fence, and went down to look at Horse the First and Horse the Second, who were still living in our barn until Mr. Archer and Grandma were more settled in their own place. Horse the Second was growing already and filling out, and you could tell he was going to be absolutely beautiful when he grew up.

John's hand rested lightly on my shoulder. "Happy now?" he asked me.

I snuggled up against him. "Yes, so happy that some-times I'm afraid it won't last."

"You don't have to be afraid of happiness, Jo," he said solemnly. "You've earned it, if anyone has."

"I didn't do very much," I said modestly. "If anyone did anything, it was Horse. Horse started everything."

"Well, Horse may have started it," John agreed, "but someone had to carry on from there, and you've made a lot of people happy, Jo, even if you did do it in rather a bungling way. Isn't that right, Horse?"

I wasn't mad because we were old friends now, and old friends could say anything to each other. As for Horse, she looked down at Horse the Second sleeping in the straw, then very deliberately she leaned against the wall, closed her eyes and went to sleep. I had never seen such a smug, self-satisfied horse in all my life.

"That's telling you," I said.

"Yes," laughed John. "I can see whose side she's on. I'll have to watch what I say in the future."

With our arms around each other, we tiptoed out of the barn, closed the door softly behind us and went back to the party.

About the Author

Diana Walker began writing at the age of eight, and had her first book published when she was seventeen. She is the author of *The Mystery of Black Gut*, *The Skiers of Ste. Celeste* (A Junior Literary Guild Selection) and *Never Step on an Indian's Shadow*, all published by Abelard-Schuman.

Diana Walker lives with her husband in Bolton, Ontario, north of Toronto, Canada. They share a great love of the wilderness and take regular trips in the Canadian north with their kayak, their tent and their dog.

In addition, as Mrs. Walker explains: "Since deciding to write a book about horses, I have taken up riding to learn something about them, and have become hooked despite many tumbles and aching muscles."